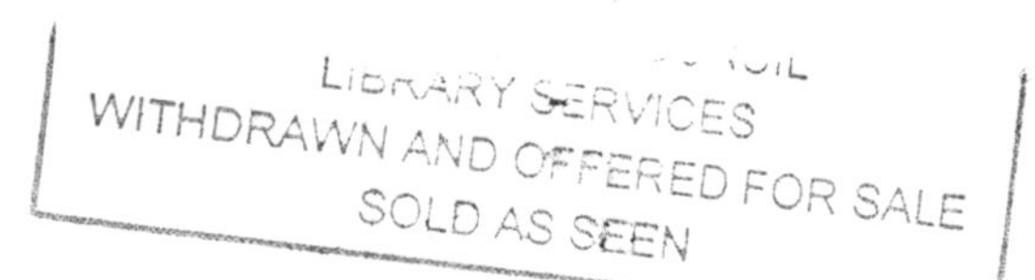

THE KISSING TREE

THE KISSING TREE

Susan Darke

Chivers Press
Bath, England
•
Thorndike Press
Waterville, Maine USA

This Large Print edition is published by Chivers Press, England, and by Thorndike Press, USA.

Published in 2003 in the U.K. by arrangement with Robert Hale Limited.

Published in 2003 in the U.S. by arrangement with Robert Hale Limited.

U.K. Hardcover ISBN 0–7540–8897–9 (Chivers Large Print)
U.K. Softcover ISBN 0–7540–8898–7 (Camden Large Print)
U.S. Softcover ISBN 0–7862–5125–5 (General Series Edition)

The text of this Large Print edition is unabridged.
Other aspects of the book may vary from the original edition.

Set in 16 pt. New Times Roman.

Printed in Great Britain on acid-free paper.

British Library Cataloguing in Publication Data available

Library of Congress Control Number: 2002115676

CHAPTER ONE

'I hate to ask you, Jenny, but could you possibly come home for a couple of weeks?' Even over the long distance telephone Jenny Clayton could detect a note of strain in her father's voice. 'Morwenna's got to go into hospital and she's worried sick about leaving Carol. In fact she says she'll put off having the operation till Carol's better but I don't want her to do that. She's already been on the waiting list for over a year.'

'Of course she mustn't put it off.' Jenny was horrified at the very idea. Her stepmother had been soldiering on for months with an ailment which gave her considerable discomfort and it would be foolhardy of her to postpone medical treatment now that a bed was available. 'I'll come home if you really think it's necessary,' she continued, 'but isn't it time Carol made some sort of effort? I'm sure she could snap out of it if she really wanted to.'

Jenny's eighteen-year-old half-sister was suffering from nervous depression and, although Jenny was sorry for the girl, she suspected she rather enjoyed being the centre of attention. As a child she had been delicate and her parents had given in to her every whim. Consequently she had grown up to be a wayward, difficult girl and, latterly, she had become a real problem to her family. It was largely because of Carol that Jenny had left home, and for the past six months she had been sharing a flat in London with a couple of other girls and working in a large health clinic.

Originally she had trained as a nurse but, shortly before her final exams, she had contracted glandular fever and, when she was better, she had been advised to take a less arduous job. This was a bitter disappointment to her because she had loved nursing, and she was still undecided what to do when Dr Hatherley, their local G.P., offered her a job as his receptionist. She worked happily for him for several months and would probably have stayed on if it hadn't been for Carol who seemed to resent her living at home, though it was difficult to understand why, because it was Jenny who always took second place. If she had been of a jealous nature she would have resented the fact that her half-sister apparently meant more to her father than she did, though Richard himself would have been horrified had he realized he treated his two daughters differently.

'Carol can't help her disposition,' he said now. 'You've never suffered from your nerves so you don't understand how difficult life is for her.'

Jenny sighed. 'All right, Dad. We won't argue about it. How soon do you want me to come home?'

'This week-end if possible—Morwenna's supposed to be going into hospital on Monday. Yes, I know it's short notice but they evidently had a last-minute cancellation.'

'Okay, I'll manage it somehow.' Jenny had a week's holiday due to her and she supposed she could take an extra week without pay. It would mean saying good-bye to the winter coat she had been saving for but it was all in a good cause. She was fond of Morwenna who had been kind to her when she was a motherless little girl and, although they didn't always see eye to eye with each other, especially over Carol, they had remained good friends.

Optimistically Richard had already looked up the times of the trains and he said he would pick Jenny up at the station at two o'clock on Saturday afternoon. 'You've taken a load off my mind,' he told her. 'Morwenna will be terribly grateful.'

'But not Carol,' Jenny thought. She didn't suppose Carol had ever been grateful to anybody in her whole life. Yet people loved her. Even Jenny loved her in a strange sort of way. She looked so fragile and vulnerable and, although she was abominably selfish and lazy, there was something about her, some mysterious appeal, which aroused the maternal instincts in women and the chivalrous instincts in men.

The phone call had come early on Friday morning and as soon as Jenny got to the clinic she went to the administration office to see about getting time off. Luckily it was a slack period, most of the staff having already had their summer holidays, so she was able to have the fortnight she asked for, though it was given to her rather grudgingly.

'We don't usually grant compassionate leave on such flimsy grounds,' Miss Prossor remarked, looking down her long, thin nose. 'It's not as if your sister is a young child. She and your father should be perfectly capable of looking after themselves while your stepmother is in hospital.'

'I know it sounds feeble,' Jenny agreed, 'but Carol is suffering from nervous depression and Dad's so clueless he can't even boil an egg.'

'Well, don't make a habit of asking for time off in order to spoon-feed your family,' Miss Prossor said. 'Remember, you've only been working at the clinic for a short time and we wouldn't have any difficulty in replacing you.'

This was only too true. Jenny's job was a purely routine one and scores of girls could have done it equally well, whereas when she was working for Dr Hatherley he had often said she was indispensable, and he had been very cut up when she told him she was leaving home and getting a job in London.

'I may have to be away longer than a fortnight,' Jenny admitted. 'It depends on how my stepmother feels when she comes out of hospital.'

'In that case I suggest you give in your notice straightaway. You can always re-apply at a later date.' Judging by her tone of voice Miss Prossor evidently thought it most unlikely that Jenny would be reinstated.

'All right. I suppose I'd better do that,' Jenny agreed rather unwillingly. She knew her father and Morwenna would be delighted to have her home again and, with any luck, she could get her old job back with Dr Hatherley. But did she really want to return? The set-up would be the same as before, with the whole household revolving round Carol. 'Perhaps I'll meet a tall, dark, handsome stranger and I'll ride away with him on his white horse,' she thought, trying to cheer herself up. But there seemed little likelihood of this happening because any boy friends she brought home made an immediate bee-line for Carol who, from a very early age, had been the possessor of that mysterious alchemy known as sex appeal.

Perhaps things would be different now. If Carol was really suffering from nervous depression she would hardly be in the right mood to captivate members of the opposite sex, especially as her depression had been triggered off by a disastrous love affair. Married, with three children, Edmund Rockford was far too old for Carol but, for some reason or other, she had taken a fancy to him and he, very foolishly had responded to her advances. He came to his senses only just in time to prevent his wife from starting divorce proceedings and the affair ended in tears and recriminations. Edmund rightly refused to have anything more to do with Carol who became wildly hysterical and threatened to commit suicide. She eventually calmed down and lapsed into a state of apathy, refusing to go to college and moping around the house like a limp rag. Privately Jenny suspected that the whole production was a form of exhibitionism and that Carol was not so much broken-hearted as upset by the fact that it was Edmund and not herself who had ended the affair. Previously it had always been Carol who had tired first and the reversal of rôles didn't suit her ladyship. How long she would keep up the charade was anybody's guess but, while it lasted, her mother and father lived in a state of continual anxiety.

Leaving London in such a hurry meant that Jenny had little time for regret. Fortunately she had already paid for her share of the flat till the end of the month but it would take most of her meagre savings to pay for a taxi to the station and her train fare home. However, the state of her finances was the least of her worries because she knew her father would reimburse her, and that she wouldn't go short of pocket money while she was out of a job. What really worried her was the prospect of running the house during Morwenna's absence and—even more alarming—looking after Carol, who from all accounts, needed attention day and night. Apparently she had started walking in her sleep and Richard and Morwenna were obliged to take it in turns to keep watch for fear the girl should come to harm.

Sleep-walking was an old habit of Carol's. As a child it had only ceased when Morwenna agreed to share a bedroom with her, leaving Richard to sleep on his own, and she was quite a big girl before she decided she wanted her bedroom to herself. This may have had something to do with the fact that Richard decorated Jenny's bedroom as a present for her thirteenth birthday and Carol didn't want to be left out. Nothing would satisfy her until her room was redecorated too, which resulted in a fortunate side effect because, when it was finished, Morwenna was allowed to sleep with Richard again and the nocturnal wanderings were forgotten.

On the journey home Jenny occupied a window seat and, as the train hurtled along through endless miles of countryside, another worry took shape in her mind. It was the first week in September, the time when the plums and the apples ripened, and the hedgerows were full of blackberries. Jenny's heart sank when she realized what lay ahead of her, because her stepmother was an absolute squirrel. At this time of year Morwenna stayed up till all hours, making jams and jellies, pickling onions and making tomato chutney and goodness knows what else, and no doubt she would expect Jenny to perform these duties for her while she was in hospital.

Jenny had never minded helping but the idea of coping on her own would have daunted a stouter heart than hers. If only Carol would pull her weight it wouldn't be so bad but, even in the old days, her sister hardly ever lifted a finger to help while, in her present state of health, presumably she would be a dead loss.

By the time the train drew into the station Jenny was feeling thoroughly despondent and, to make matters worse, her father wasn't there to meet her. She gave up her ticket at the barrier and putting down her suitcase she wondered how long she would have to wait. Her father was usually very punctual but it was a twenty-mile drive from the village and anything could have happened to delay him.

Several minutes elapsed before she realized that a lone man was hovering in the vicinity, obviously debating whether he should speak to her. In response to her half smile he came forward and asked her if she was Jenny Clayton.

'I'm Nigel Barrett,' he explained. 'I told your father I'd give you a lift.' Jenny was about to thank him when he cut her short. 'I was coming into town in any case and it seemed unnecessary for us both to make the journey.'

'Do you live near us?' Jenny asked as she got into the car. Certainly Nigel Barrett was a new face. Having lived in the village all her life she was on nodding acquaintance with most of the inhabitants, but she realized there would have been changes during her six months absence.

'I'm Doctor Hatherley's locum,' he explained. 'I'm looking after your sister while he's away, so I call in most days to see her.'

'Even on Saturdays? She's surely not ill enough to take up so much of your time?'

'I find her an interesting case,' he answered. 'Doctor Hatherley hasn't made much progress with his treatment, so I'm hoping I shall come up with the right answer.'

'I shouldn't take Carol too seriously—she'll bob up again in her own good time,' Jenny assured him, but her flippant remark didn't go down very well with the new doctor.

'Psychiatry is a closed book to those who haven't made a study of the subject,' he declared. 'Your sister needs love and understanding during this difficult period.'

'Part of Carol's trouble is that she's been smothered with love all her life and she's thoroughly spoilt,' Jenny retorted. 'Believe me, I know what I'm talking about.'

Disapproval was written all over Nigel Barrett's countenance and the next few miles were covered in complete silence. Then Jenny made an effort to communicate. After all, he couldn't be blamed if Carol was making a fool of him. Given time he would see the girl in her true colours. So, for the rest of the journey, she made trivial conversation about the weather and the crops and country life in general and, although she didn't get much response, they didn't end up by quarrelling with one another.

'Thanks for the lift,' she said, as she got out of the car. 'I won't ask you to come in because I'm sure you've been delayed enough already.'

'You won't forget what I said about being kind to your sister?' Nigel repeated as he handed her her suitcase. 'I get the feeling you aren't the best of friends and this so often happens in families. The trouble stems from childhood jealousy and over the years it builds up out of all proportion.'

Jenny saw red. 'I have read Freud, you know,' she responded acidly, 'and for your information I did part of my nurse's training in a mental hospital. If you think for one moment that Carol is genuinely suffering from depression I warn you you are making a big mistake. Incidentally, if you have leanings towards being a psychiatrist, whatever made you become a G.P.? In this village, at any rate, you'll be far too busy dealing with gall bladders and babies and other basics to spare the time for trick cycling.'

With which parting shot she turned on her heel and hurried up the path, angry with herself for letting him get under her skin.

She received a loving welcome from Richard and Morwenna and they were delighted when she told them she had packed in her job and would be staying at home for as long as she was needed.

'That's splendid news!' Richard exclaimed. 'But are you quite sure it's what you want to do? We don't want to spoil your plans, and you were so eager to go to London.'

Jenny pulled a face. 'I wasn't all that keen,' she admitted. 'I just thought it would be a good idea to leave the nest but, honestly, I'm thankful to be home again. I'm too much of a country cousin to be happy in the Big City and, to be perfectly truthful, I didn't like being a little fish in a big ocean. Here at home everybody knows me and cares about me and I'm "somebody" instead of "nobody".'

Richard laughed and gave her a hug. '"East, West, home's best",' he quoted.

'Do you think Doctor Hatherley will have me back again?' Jenny asked. 'I don't mean straightaway but when Morwenna's better.'

'Yes, I'm sure he will. The girl he's got at the moment isn't very satisfactory and in any case she's leaving shortly to get married. He was only saying to me the other day how much he misses you.'

'I gather he's on holiday at the moment,' Jenny remarked. 'What do you think of his locum?'

'He's absolutely wonderful.' Morwenna's pale face lit up momentarily. 'Carol likes him and I'm convinced that, if anyone can effect a cure, it's Doctor Barrett.'

'Actually I can't think why you didn't send her to a nerve specialist long ago,' Jenny remarked. 'He would soon have sorted her out.'

'Doctor Hatherley did suggest it but Carol refused point-blank. That's why it's so marvellous that Doctor Barrett is interested in psychiatry. It's much less traumatic to be seen by a G.P. than a specialist, and Carol seems to enjoy his visits.'

'Yes,' thought Jenny. 'I'm not surprised. He's extremely good-looking and she knows he won't cotton on to the fact that she's a fraud as quickly as a specialist would.'

But Jenny herself was shocked by Carol's appearance when she went upstairs to say 'hullo' to her. Her sister had always been on the thin side but now she was positively skinny, though she was still beautiful. She was the sort of person, Jenny thought half enviously, who would look beautiful when she was quite old, for she was the lucky possessor of perfect bone structure, and her eyes were that incredible deep blue so rarely encountered. She had inherited them from Richard but, curiously enough, in a man they were less noticeable. 'Just my luck to miss out on the right genes,' Jenny often sighed, 'and inherit all the bad points from my parents.' Living with Carol had given her an inferiority complex and her mirror-reflection never told her the truth about herself, so she had no idea she was the possessor of a lovely smile, that she walked straight and tall and that, even on dull days, the sunlight lingered in her hair.

'What are you doing lying in bed at this time of day?' she demanded, coming straight to the point. She had decided that the best way to bring Carol back to normal was to stop wrapping her in cotton wool, and she saw no reason to change her tactics just because her sister looked like death warmed up. 'If you've got to rest why don't you sit in the garden?'

Carol gave a delicate shudder. 'I couldn't possibly do that,' she answered. 'Doctor Barrett says I'm suffering from agoraphobia. I don't suppose you know what that is, but it's a fear of open spaces.'

'For crying out loud!' Jenny exclaimed. 'It's not as if the garden's a prairie—it's only about thirty square yards and it's surrounded by fruit trees and a fence. Get your clothes on, girl, and come downstairs. I'll hold your hand if it makes you feel any safer.'

'I don't want to,' Carol pouted. 'I wish you hadn't come home if all you're going to do is bully me.'

'Don't be like that,' Jenny coaxed. 'It's a lovely afternoon and it seems a shame to waste it indoors. Remember there isn't much summer left for us to enjoy.'

'I'll get up by and by and watch television,' Carol answered. 'Meanwhile I'd be obliged if you'll leave me in peace. You've already given me a headache, bursting into the room like a bull in a china shop and throwing your weight about. You look so disgustingly healthy.'

'It's much more disgusting to be an invalid,' Jenny retorted, 'especially as there's really nothing the matter with you. Own up, Carol. Isn't this just a big act to make people feel sorry for you? I believe you're enjoying every minute of it, and you couldn't be more chuffed now that Doctor Barrett has appeared on the scene.'

'I don't know how you can be so cruel,' Carol protested, her lovely eyes filling with tears. 'I knew it was a mistake letting Daddy ask you to come home and look after me, but I didn't think you'd start picking on me the moment you arrived. I'll tell Mummy I can't stand it and I know she'll put off going into hospital until I'm better.'

Jenny lost her temper. 'Of all the selfish little toads,' she exclaimed. 'Honestly, Carol, you just about take the biscuit. Look,' she added more gently, 'I'm sorry if I upset you but I don't think you realise how wretchedly ill Morwenna feels, and you haven't helped matters by choosing to play up at this particular time.'

'I didn't *choose* for Edmund to break my

heart,' Carol responded sulkily.

'Was he really that important to you?' Jenny asked. 'A middle-aged man, with a wife and three children? I wouldn't have thought you would have looked twice at him. Now, if it had been *me.*' She gave a self-derisive smile. 'But then—I've never been surrounded by eager suitors. Carol, darling, please make an effort for Morwenna's sake, if not your own. You owe it to her to let her have peace of mind before she goes into hospital.'

'Well, I don't know what you expect me to do,' Carol grumbled. 'Pretend I've had a miraculous recovery? You don't know how awful I feel. The moment I put a foot out of bed I feel weak and giddy.'

'That's only because you've been starving yourself,' Jenny declared. 'It's easy to get into the habit of not eating properly. When you were a little girl you used it as a weapon to get your own way. Yes—I saw through you all right. Like the sleep walking and everything else. But you're grown up now, Carol, and it's time you learnt self-discipline—and self-respect. Well, that's the end of my little sermon.' She leaned over and kissed her sister's pale cheek. 'I love you, Carol, but love shows itself in different ways and I won't pander to you, like Morwenna does. And I'm afraid Dad's just as foolish.'

Carol's lips trembled. 'I *want* to get better,' she whispered.

'Then the battle's half won,' Jenny replied. 'Suppose you let me help you get dressed and you can give everybody a nice surprise by coming downstairs to tea.'

Jenny's tactics paid dividends and, for the first time in many weeks, Carol joined the family for a meal instead of having it in her room. She ate very little and clearly considered Jenny was slightly vulgar to tuck into her food with such gusto. However, although her contribution to the conversation was negligible, she did condescend to answer when she was spoken to instead of sitting in total silence.

'She's being so brave, bless her,' Morwenna remarked to Jenny later that evening. 'She knows how much I dread leaving her and she's doing her best to make it easy for me.' There followed a long list of instructions to which Jenny listened patiently and, characteristically, Morwenna spent the next day busily making plans for the comfort of her whole family —and of Carol in particular—instead of preparing herself for the ordeal that lay ahead of her.

'This business of going into hospital couldn't have come at a worse time,' she mourned. 'What with Carol so poorly and the plums almost ready for picking. Could you, Jenny? Would you? I hate to ask you, but . . .'

'All right, Wenna,' Jenny agreed, half laughing. 'I won't let your wretched plums rot on the ground. I'll hand pick them and make hundreds of pounds of jam for you to give away to jumble sales and other charities.'

'Don't tease, Jenny. You know I like a well-stocked larder and, since we bought the big chest freezer, nothing need go to waste. I'll show you how to prepare the fruit and pack it into convenient sized freezer bags. It's really not a lot of trouble if you do it in big batches.'

Jenny had half hoped there wouldn't be a bumper crop of plums this year but her hopes were soon dashed. She remembered the beautiful blossom hanging like snow on the three sturdy trees at the bottom of the garden, and, at a rough estimate she reckoned there would be more than sixty pounds on every tree. With such a mammoth task ahead of her she was relieved that the apples wouldn't be ready for another week or two, but already there were windfalls and these would have to be attended to regularly. 'Oh, for a handy orphanage,' she sighed. 'As far as I'm concerned the children could have the lot—maggots included.' But Morwenna reminded her that the windfalls—peeled, cored and de-maggotted—made the most delicious apple fool.

'Don't you remember?' she asked. 'When you were a little girl you demanded apple fool for breakfast, dinner, tea and supper. I must say it was always a pleasure to see you tucking in at mealtimes and I often wonder why Carol was so fussy, but of course she's always been delicate, poor child.'

'Wenna, I don't want to criticize, but do you think she really was all that delicate? I mean, she was never *really* ill, was she, although she was always missing school on some pretence or other.'

'You mean I spoilt her? Yes, I suppose I did.' This was the first time that Morwenna had ever admitted she might have made mistakes in her child's upbringing. 'I don't expect you to understand, Jenny, and you were too young to remember, but I nearly died when Carol was born, and I was told I could never have another baby, so she was terribly precious to me.'

'Yes, I do understand,' Jenny answered, and it was to her credit that she spoke without bitterness. 'If you'd lost her you'd only have had me, and that wouldn't have compensated because I'm not a part of you, like Carol is. I suppose that's why you treated us differently. Not that I'm complaining,' she added. 'You've always been sweet to me, although I'm only your stepdaughter, and thank goodness you didn't smother me with love.'

She didn't add 'or I might have turned out like Carol' because she had said enough already. She could only hope that her mild criticism would have some effect. Then perhaps, in future, Morwenna might realize there was some truth in the saying that you must sometimes be cruel to be kind.

That night she slept with her bedroom door ajar, having told Richard and Morwenna she would be responsible for Carol. As far as she could ascertain they hadn't slept together since their daughter became ill, and she felt they were entitled to a 'honeymoon' night before their enforced parting. But, as it turned out, she wasn't disturbed. Rather cynically she wondered if this was because Carol knew she would get short shrift from her hard-hearted sister if she indulged in her nocturnal prowlings but, to give her the benefit of the doubt, perhaps the quiet night indicated she was taking the first step along the road to recovery.

Richard, who was a solicitor, had taken the day off in order to drive Morwenna to the hospital and he visited her again during the afternoon and evening. Jenny tried to persuade Carol to go with him but the girl burst into tears at the very suggestion.

'You *know* I can't go out,' she sobbed, 'and it would *kill* me to go inside the hospital. I simply couldn't stand it.'

'What is it you're supposed to be suffering from?' Jenny retorted. 'Agoraphobia or claustrophobia? It sounds like a mixture of both. Come off it, Carol. Aren't you going to visit Morwenna all the time she's in hospital?'

'Mummy understands. I'll write to her of course.'

Jenny snorted. 'Big deal!' she exclaimed. 'I'm sure that will be a great comfort to her!' She wished Carol would stop calling her parents 'Mummy and Daddy'. At eighteen, going on nineteen, it was high time she grew up but it seemed that she wanted to be child and woman at one and the same time and, by so doing, get the best of both worlds.

'Well, if you won't go you won't and that's the end of it, I suppose,' she continued. 'But I'm not going to have you moping indoors all afternoon. You'd better come into the garden and hold the ladder while I pick some plums.'

So, when Nigel Barrett turned up around teatime, he found them enjoying the sunshine out of doors. He had received no reply to his ring at the front door and, thinking that Carol was probably resting, he wandered round to the back garden on the off-chance of finding Jenny. He feared that, with Morwenna in hospital, his patient might be neglected and he wanted to stress how important it was for Carol to have plenty of loving attention.

He thought the two girls made a delightful picture, with Jenny perched high on the ladder and Carol reaching up for the laden basket. She was wearing a cotton skirt and sleeveless blouse and she looked quite different from the wan little invalid who had been causing him such concern.

'How nice to see you up and about, Miss Clayton,' he remarked. 'But you mustn't overdo it.' And he held out his hand for the basket which Carol was still clutching. She hadn't expected Nigel to call until later because he had told her he would be tied up all afternoon, and she had planned to be indoors long before his visit. Now she was caught out and she had to hide her discomfiture as best she could.

'Jenny *made* me,' she pouted. 'She was afraid she might fall off the ladder and break a leg.'

'I doubt if your sister has ever been afraid of anything,' Nigel remarked dryly and, from the way he spoke, it didn't sound like a compliment.

'We were just going to have tea,' Jenny said rather ungraciously. 'Would you like to stop or are you in too much of a rush?'

'That would be nice,' he answered, glancing at his watch. 'I have to make some evening calls but there's no hurry.'

'Then I'll go and put on the kettle.' She took the basket from him and absent-mindedly popped a plum into her mouth. Seeing the look on his face she told him to help himself. 'But don't let Carol eat any more,' she warned. 'She's been pigging them up all the afternoon.'

'I *haven't*,' Carol protested, justifiably incensed by this slur on her character, but Jenny only laughed.

'Chairs are in the summerhouse,' she told Nigel. 'It's so lovely we might as well have tea in the garden.'

When she came out again ten minutes later, bearing a laden tray, Carol and Nigel were comfortably ensconced in the shade of the apple tree. A little pile of plum stones was neatly arranged on the picnic table and Jenny flicked them on one side. 'She loves me, she don't, she'll marry me, she won't,' she chanted. 'Too bad, Doctor Barrett. That's what comes of being greedy and eating four plums instead of three.'

'*I* ate the other one,' Carol interposed quickly, 'so it doesn't count. Anyway, it's all a silly old superstition: like peeling an apple and throwing the peel over your shoulder to find out the name of the person you're going to marry.'

Jenny laughed. 'But we always do it, don't we, Carol? Even though we don't believe in it. Are you superstitious, Doctor Barrett?'

'No, I can't say I am,' he replied, rather stiffly. 'In my opinion it's all a lot of mumbo-jumbo.'

'There speaks a man with a scientific mind,' Jenny remarked. 'Heigh ho! I must say I'm disappointed. When I first met you I thought you bore all the hallmarks of a witch doctor.'

She was being deliberately flippant, in the forlorn hope that Dr Barrett might be persuaded to drop his professional manner and, after he had taken his departure, Carol rolled her eyes heavenward. 'If that's the way you treat your boy friends, no wonder you can't see them for dust,' she exclaimed.

'I would hardly call Nigel Barrett my boy friend,' Jenny pointed out. 'I thought you'd already staked your claim and you're more than welcome. Of all the stuffed shirts I've ever met he takes the prize. Thank goodness he's only a locum, so when I start work with Doctor Hatherley, I shan't have to put up with him bossing me about.'

'I think perhaps you will,' Carol answered a trifle smugly. 'He's seriously contemplating going into partnership with Doctor Hatherley.'

Jenny stared at her open-mouthed. 'In heaven's name—why?' she asked. 'What attraction can a village like this have for him? I would have thought he'd got his sights firmly fixed on Harley Street. Or, more likely, *Wimpole* Street. He's even got the right name for it. Doctor Barrett of Wimpole Street. How very appropriate!'

And, with an unladylike giggle, she picked up the tray and led the way indoors.

CHAPTER TWO

Morwenna made very good progress after her operation and, when she came out of hospital on the tenth day, she was looking much more herself again. All the same Jenny insisted on staying home for another fortnight so that her stepmother could convalesce in comfort. In any case, Dr Hatherley's present Girl Friday wanted to stay on till the end of the month, so it was the beginning of October before Jenny started work at the surgery. By this time Nigel Barrett was fairly well acquainted with the running of the practice and was on good terms with most of the patients, some of whom were happy to welcome a younger man, though others were more conservative and invariably asked to see the 'old' doctor.

When Jenny turned up at the surgery on her first morning he greeted her without enthusiasm, but this was hardly surprising. She knew he hadn't been best pleased to hear she was going to work for Dr Hatherley and she realized this was partly her own fault. Tact had never been her strong point and he was annoyed with her for refusing to take Carol's illness seriously. Consequently there were continual clashes between them, but Jenny was determined not to molly-coddle her sister just to please him.

In point of fact there had been a marked improvement in Carol's condition since Jenny's return, but Dr Barrett got all the credit for it, and she was getting sick and tired of hearing Morwenna and Richard sing his praises.

'You're five minutes late,' he said reprovingly as she hung her coat on the hook behind the door and put on her neat blue overall. 'If there's one thing I dislike it's unpunctuality.'

She stifled the impulse to drop him a curtsy and say: 'Sorry, *sir.*' Instead she murmured a polite apology and assured him it wouldn't happen again. But she couldn't help resenting his attitude. She had a perfectly valid reason for being late because Morwenna had twisted her ankle coming downstairs to breakfast, and she had had to stop and bandage it before leaving. She could have explained this to Dr Hatherley and, in any case, *he* wouldn't have reprimanded her, but Dr Barrett's frigid manner was very off-putting and he would be sure to think she was just making a feeble excuse.

'There's a lot to do before surgery,' he continued. 'For a start all the case histories have to be sorted through. I can't think why the last girl let them get into such a muddle—they aren't even in alphabetical order.'

A brief glance showed Jenny that her efficient filing system had gone completely haywire. No wonder Dr Hatherley had welcomed her back with open arms. It would take most the morning to put things right and, in between times, she would have to answer the telephone and try to catch up with a mountain of neglected correspondence to the local health authority. She would also have to be on hand to help with minor casualties, thus taking some of the load off the shoulders of whichever doctor was on duty.

But Dr Barrett wasn't Dr Hatherley and he told her in no uncertain terms that he preferred to have his consulting-room to himself.

'By all means feel free to assist Doctor Hatherley if he wants you to,' he said, 'but my methods are somewhat different.'

'Very well, Doctor Barrett,' she replied, her eyes flashing. 'If you are too high and mighty to accept my help just because I'm not fully qualified, it's your own affair. Far be it from me to point out that the waiting-room is full to bursting and that, without my assistance, it will be difficult to get through the morning's work in time for lunch.'

He gave her an ironic glance. 'I have been managing quite well without your assistance for the past month,' he reminded her. 'In any case it has nothing whatever to do with your qualifications, though, since you've brought up the subject yourself, I may say I think it's a great pity you opted out of nursing before taking your final exams.' He knew nothing about her long illness and the fact that she had been strongly advised by Dr Hatherley not to continue with her chosen career, so the injustice of this remark left her speechless. However, he apparently didn't notice she had almost reached boiling point. 'I don't want to make too many changes all at once,' he continued, 'but I'm hoping to persuade Doctor Hatherley to adopt the appointments system. It's far more efficient than this haphazard way of letting patients turn up at whatever time they please.'

She hung on to her temper with the greatest difficulty. 'I doubt if such a system would be very popular in a country practice like this,' she argued. 'In any case, why bother to make changes if you aren't going to stay?'

Carol had been wrong in supposing that Dr Barrett intended going into partnership with Dr Hatherley. In point of fact he was only staying on as his assistant for a few months before taking up the post of Houseman in a London hospital. 'As a stepping stone to Wimpole Street,' Jenny surmised, and she thought that such a job would be far more suited to his temperament than a country practice. 'He's more interested in *cases* than people,' she decided.

But in this she did him less than justice and she soon realized that his rather brusque manner was a cover for what was basically a compassionate nature. She still thought he was unbearably opinionated and dogmatic at times but she had to admit that he was kindness itself to those who genuinely needed his help.

One particular occasion stuck in her mind when an elderly patient fainted after having an injection and, although he was extremely busy, with Dr Hatherley off sick and a tight schedule for the rest of the day, he took her into the kitchen and asked Mrs Hatherley to give her a cup of tea and chat with her until he was free to drive her home, instead of letting her wait around for a bus.

On the other hand he had no patience with malingerers and the word soon got around that you couldn't pull wool over the young doctor's eyes. Consequently, while many of the patients were content to see whichever doctor was on duty, others unfailingly turned up when they could be sure they would be treated by Dr Hatherley, and Jenny derived considerable quiet amusement from the way in which the sheep sorted themselves out from the goats.

Another point in Dr Barrett's favour was his consideration for the older man. Until recently Dr Hatherley had managed the practice on his own but latterly his health hadn't been too good and, when he returned from his holiday, he was pleased to accept his locum's offer to stay on for a while. Dr Barrett asked Jenny to co-operate with him in ensuring that he himself dealt with the more distant calls. It was a scattered practice and many of the farms and cottages were isolated and not very get-at-able. To someone suffering from chronic bronchitis even a short walk over rough countryside in bad weather was asking for trouble. 'But please be tactful about it,' he insisted. 'I don't want Doctor Hatherley to think I'm taking over from him.'

It had already been arranged that the older doctor should do the morning round and evening surgery, while his assistant took morning surgery and the afternoon round. The practice covered a wide area, which meant that Nigel was invariably busy until the early part of the evening and, as he also insisted on being on call at night from eleven o'clock onwards, his time for social pursuits was strictly limited. Not that this appeared to worry him. He was a great reader and Jenny was more than a little impressed by the sort of books he studied.

'I've never known such a man for keeping his nose to the grindstone,' she thought. 'It's almost as if he's using work as a drug to help himself forget some tragedy. I wonder if he's had an unhappy love affair.'

'Yes,' she decided. 'Perhaps that's what's the matter with him.' It would account for a number of things. His dedication to work. His unfriendly attitude towards herself. His complete disinterest in women except where his patients were concerned. Still, his private life was none of her business and she quickly stifled her curiosity. In any case, she wasn't particularly interested in his affairs.

However, she pricked up her ears when he casually mentioned he was related to the Wickham family who lived on one of the outlying farms. 'I didn't realize Cynthia and Alan were your cousins,' she said, immediately feeling more friendlily disposed towards him.

'I went to school with Cynthia and I remember having a terrific crush on Alan when I was about fifteen. We spent the whole of one summer holiday more or less in each other's pockets. Then he went away to an agricultural college and I never saw him again.'

'Oh—Alan!' Nigel exclaimed, rather disparagingly. 'He was always one for the girls.'

'What's he doing now?' she asked. Although Jenny had got over her schoolgirl crush a long time ago she still had tender memories of the handsome young Wickham boy. 'Don't tell me he's married and settled down.'

'No, he still lives at the farm. My aunt and uncle died several years ago and Cynthia has since married. Perhaps you remember Guy Morris? He went to the grammar school but he was more my contemporary than Alan's. They run the farm between them now, and Cynthia is wife, housekeeper and general dogsbody. Hard work but she seems to thrive on it.'

Jenny stared. 'Did you go to the grammar school too?' she asked. 'I had no idea you used to live in these parts. Somehow I'd got it fixed in my head that you came from London.'

'No, I'm a real country bumpkin.' He was in a more relaxed mood than usual and actually smiled at her as if she was a human being instead of something the cat had brought in. 'My father was in practice only a few miles from here, so I know this neck of the woods like the back of my hand.'

'I suppose that's why you answered Doctor Hatherley's advertisement for a locum? I must say I was more than a little surprised when I first saw you, because the locums who come here are usually in their dotage.'

'I'm surprised to hear it,' he said dryly. 'I haven't found these past few weeks exactly a rest cure. But I enjoy the work. I like the personal involvement that comes from getting to know the patients as human beings instead of case histories, going into their homes and meeting their families. It's very much more rewarding than the conveyor-belt system practised in hospitals.'

Jenny's eyes widened. This statement didn't tally with her preconceived notion of his interests. 'Yet that's where your future lies,' she remarked.

'Yes, I suppose so. Originally I intended going into partnership with my father but, after my mother died, he decided to fulfil a lifelong ambition and see the world, so he sold his practice and became a ship's doctor. Probably just as well from my point of view or I might have settled into a nice, comfortable rut at far too early an age. As it is I shall have to learn to stand on my own two feet. Being an S.H.O. at a large teaching hospital will be good experience and eventually I shall probably apply for a consultancy in a psychiatric hospital, because I've always been interested in mental diseases. Meanwhile it suits me very well to stay on as Doctor Hatherley's assistant. The pay's not particularly good but I get free board and lodging, and it's conveniently near to the Wickhams, which is the main reason why I took the job. Alan and I have always been at odds with each other but I get on very well with Guy, and I look on Cynthia more as a sister than a cousin.'

'I'd like to meet up with her again,' Jenny said impulsively. 'It's ages since I last saw her.' Seeing Nigel's slightly raised eyebrows she had the grace to blush. 'All right,' she owned. 'I'd like to see Alan. Not that he would remember me.'

'Probably not,' was the rather dampening reply. 'There have been so many girls in Alan's life he's probably lost count of half of them. But don't let me put you off. If you'd really like to meet the Wickhams again there's no reason why you shouldn't. As a matter of fact I shall be spending the day with them next Sunday and I don't mind taking you with me.'

An invitation from Nigel! Wonders would never cease! Jenny hid her astonishment as best she could. 'I couldn't just land myself on Cynthia without so much as a "by your leave",' she protested.

'Why not? It's always been open house at the Wickhams and one extra mouth to feed won't make much difference.'

'Then—*thanks*. That'll be absolutely super.'

The rest of the week dragged by but Sunday came at last and, as Jenny settled herself into the passenger seat of Nigel's car, she was conscious of a mounting excitement at the prospect of meeting Alan again. She could call him to mind quite vividly, though she had only been a schoolgirl when she last saw him. Tall and dark and more than usually handsome, even as a boy he had stood out in a crowd, and her heartbeats quickened when she remembered that wonderful summer holiday when they had gone everywhere together. Older than she was by nearly two years he was already almost a man, and it had pleased him to have her tagging along after him . . . looking up to him . . . putting him on a pedestal. He had taught her to ride, to climb trees, to fish, to swim in the ice-cold river, and he had teased or praised her according to his mood, happy in the knowledge that, however he treated her, she would remain his willing slave. Looking back, it was strange how quickly he had faded out of her life, but it was a case of out of sight, out of mind. Alan went away to an agricultural college and, when she and Cynthia left school, they lost touch with each other, so the break was inevitable.

'You're very quiet,' Nigel remarked as they neared the farm. 'Has the cat got hold of your tongue?' He was accustomed to Jenny chattering away non-stop and today's silence was so unusual it called for comment.

'I'm sorry,' she apologized. 'I'm afraid my thoughts were elsewhere.' With an effort she brought herself back to earth again. 'The farm looks prosperous,' she said, noticing the newly-roofed barns and outbuildings. 'I remember it being rather run-down and ramshackle.'

'My uncle was one of the old die-hards and he wouldn't move with the times,' Nigel replied, 'but Guy is more business-like and, since he and Cynthia got married, he's modernized the whole place.'

'That must have cost a pretty packet,' Jenny remarked. 'Where did the money come from?'

'Oh, there are always ways and means,' Nigel told her, rather vaguely. 'I think he applied for a government grant and, of course, the more efficient you are the greater the rewards. If Alan had had to shoulder the responsibility the whole place would have gone to rack and ruin. From what Cynthia tells me Guy does all the work and Alan is content to sit back and reap the benefit.'

Jenny didn't like the turn the conversation was taking and she fell silent. It disturbed her to learn that her idol had feet of clay but she decided to wait and see for herself before she passed judgement. After all, it was only natural for a wife to sing her husband's praises and it was quite possible that Cynthia had given Nigel a garbled version of the true situation. Even in the old days there hadn't been much love lost between brother and sister and evidently the years between had done little to improve their relationship.

Parking the car on the grass verge, Nigel pushed open the wooden gate and led the way round to the back of the house, along a flagged passage and into the kitchen where Cynthia was lifting a batch of freshly baked cakes out of the oven. She greeted Nigel with a loving kiss and she made Jenny equally welcome even though she hadn't been expecting an extra guest.

'Lovely to see you,' she smiled. 'Stay and talk to me while I finish peeling the sprouts. Nigel, I'm not going to stand on ceremony with you—you'll find Guy and Alan somewhere around, or you can sit down and relax if you'd rather. I expect you've had a busy week.'

Nigel helped himself to a hot cake and ambled off to look for Guy and his cousin, leaving the two girls to gossip about old times.

The kitchen, like the rest of the old house, had been modernized and all the equipment was up-to-date, but Jenny missed the old-fashioned range and the plump, motherly form of Mrs Wickham. However, she and Cynthia soon got talking, and they reminisced happily about their schooldays.

'Then you're not married yet, Jenny?' the older girl remarked. 'You ought to try it—I, for one, can thoroughly recommend it. Mind you, I know I'm lucky. Guy's a man in a thousand.'

'I'm longing to meet him,' Jenny answered. 'Nigel says he was at the grammar school so I daresay I knew him by sight though not by name.'

'I rather doubt it,' Cynthia replied. 'Guy's several years older than we are—more Nigel's age. What a crush you had on Alan. Personally I can't imagine what the girls see in him, but I suppose that's because I'm his sister.' While she was talking she tipped a colander full of sprouts into a saucepan of boiling water and she asked Jenny to keep an eye on the dinner while she went upstairs to re-do her face before dishing up. 'I expect you think I'm daft,' she remarked, 'but I'm not going to let my standards slip just because I'm married. Mum always looked as red as a turkey-cock at mealtimes and Dad never seemed to notice, but Guy's not like that.' She laughed. 'Oh, I know there's not much competition around here but I'd rather be on the safe side.'

So Jenny was alone in the kitchen when the back door opened and Alan came in. He kicked off his muddy wellington boots and, as he straightened up, he caught sight of her standing in front of the Aga stove. He obviously hadn't a clue who she was but he raised a hand in greeting. 'Hi!' he said.

He was just as she remembered him. Tall and good-looking, with the same crop of dark hair and laughing eyes. The previous evening, knowing that she was going to see him again, she had rummaged through her snapshot album and come across an old signed photograph he had given her when they were children. Memories had flooded back, bringing to mind their secret meetings, the simple pleasures they had shared, the dawning of first love. And now, as she looked at the real-life Alan, very much more mature but in essence the same, her old feelings of love and adoration took possession of her and she stood tongue-tied in front of him.

'Hi!' he said again, and added the old cliché: 'Surely we've met some place before?'

'I'm Jenny Clayton, an old schoolfriend of Cynthia's,' she answered, trying not to show how upset she was that he had forgotten her.

'And we used to play games together? Blind man's buff and kiss-in-the-ring?' He was teasing and she felt her colour rise.

'Something like that,' she admitted self-consciously. 'It was along time ago.'

'Too long,' he remarked, his bold eyes appraising her. 'What lucky chance brings you back into my life again?'

'I came with your cousin,' she explained. 'I work for Doctor Hatherley and when Nigel told me he was coming to see you I angled for an invitation.'

He raised an eyebrow. 'What a turn up for the book,' he laughed. 'I didn't think Nigel was on speaking terms with the female sex. I sincerely hope he isn't going to get ideas about you. Perhaps I'd better let him know I have a prior claim.'

'I don't think he classes me as a female,' Jenny admitted, wishing she didn't blush so easily. 'As far as he's concerned I'm just a robot.'

'A very decorative one, if I may say so.'

Jenny's flush deepened. The compliment was glib but it was none the less welcome because not many compliments had floated her way of late, especially during the past month when she had had to put up with a good deal of fault finding from Nigel.

Cynthia came into the kitchen in time to hear Alan's last remark. 'Don't listen to his blarney,' she warned, but her advice fell on deaf ears. All through dinner Jenny had eyes and ears for no one but Alan, and it was a sore disappointment to her when he pushed back his chair and excused himself, saying that he had a pressing previous engagement which he couldn't break.

After he had gone Guy and Cynthia exchanged glances. 'Hilary Carfax, I presume,' Cynthia remarked. 'Well, she's an improvement on some others I could name, so let's hope he doesn't tire of her as quickly as the last girl.'

Jenny knew the remark was made for her benefit but she pretended not to hear. Of course Alan had girl friends. Only a ninny would expect a man of his temperament to live the life of a monk and she certainly wasn't going to be put off by a detailed list of his past and present conquests. All the same it was a pity he had fixed up to see this girl Hilary on this particular afternoon. If he had known Jenny was coming he would probably have arranged to be free, but now she had no one to keep her company, because Nigel proposed to go fishing and Guy had some paper work to catch up with.

'I'm afraid I can't be much use to you either,' Cynthia apologized when they had finished washing up. 'I'm going to put my feet up for an hour. Doctor's orders,' she added, seeing Jenny's look of surprise. 'I'm having a baby next April and I've already had two miscarriages so I've been told to be careful. We're hoping it will be third time lucky.'

'Oh, I do hope so.' Jenny gave her friend a hug. 'I'll start knitting straightaway—I hope you won't mind a lop-sided matinée jacket but I'm absolutely clueless about following a pattern. Don't worry about me—I'll be quite happy wandering around on my own.

'So what do I do to amuse myself?' she thought a shade disconsolately. 'Oh, well, I suppose it's my own fault for being an uninvited guest.'

She remembered the lay-out of the farm from the old days, and presently she made her way to the stables where she found Guy, who had got through his paper work quicker than he expected. He was leading one of the horses round the yard and he greeted her with a friendly smile. A thick-set, stocky man, no one could have mistaken him for anything but a farmer, and she liked his direct glance and forthright way of speaking. He was clearly a man to be trusted, one who could be relied on in an emergency and who would be held in respect by all who knew him. Lucky Cynthia to have found the right man in the right job!

Jenny had already stopped to admire the horses who were grazing in the paddock, enjoying their Sunday rest, and she wondered why this particular horse had been segregated from the others.

'He's had a leg injury and I'm checking up to see if he's still lame,' Guy told her. 'I'm hoping to ride him in the point-to-point next Saturday.'

'He looks very high-spirited,' she ventured. 'What's his name?'

'Baronet,' he answered, and she stepped fearlessly forward and held out her hand for the horse to nuzzle. He was a fine animal, strong and well-muscled, and his coat was a lovely dark chestnut. 'No wonder Guy is proud of him,' she thought, and she had the feeling that horse and master were two of a kind.

Seeing she had no fear of Baronet, Guy asked her if she could ride and she told him Alan had taught her years ago when she was still at school. 'Cynthia's mare could do with some exercise or she'll get fat and lazy,' he remarked. 'How about having a ride on her this afternoon?'

'I'll probably fall off but I don't mind having a go if you'll promise not to laugh,' Jenny replied and Guy assured her that Sweet Briar was as gentle as a lamb. 'It would be easier to fall off a rocking horse,' he told her.

Although it was over six years since Jenny had last been on a horse she put up a fairly creditable performance. To start with she was rather tense and sat with her back held rigidly straight and her elbows tucked in, but she soon relaxed and began to enjoy herself.

Riding a horse was the ideal way to see the farm. Most of the fields were already ploughed in readiness for the autumn sowing but the mangolds and sugar beet had still to be harvested and, while they jogged along at a comfortable pace, Guy explained to her about the rotation of crops and various other facts about farming which he thought might interest her.

When they got back to the house Cynthia had had her rest and she was preparing a substantial tea despite the fact that they had all overeaten at dinner. Nigel still hadn't returned from his fishing trip and, while Guy saw to the horses, Jenny helped Cynthia spread the home-made scones with honey and clotted cream. 'Put the honey on first and the cream on top,' Cynthia said. 'It tastes much better that way.'

Jenny was so hungry after her ride that she sampled one. 'So they do,' she agreed. 'I wonder why? If the menfolk don't hurry I shall scoff the lot.'

Cynthia glanced out of the window. 'I can see Nigel coming now,' she observed. 'How do you get on with him, Jenny?'

'Fair to moderate. Let me put it like this. We aren't exactly at war but we seem to live in a state of armed truce. At any moment I expect battle to commence.'

Cynthia sighed. 'When I saw you getting out of his car this morning I hoped perhaps he was getting over Gwen Ashcott at last, and taking notice of a girl again. But I soon saw my mistake. He was so off-hand with you he was almost rude. And then, to push off all the afternoon and leave you to your own devices! I could have *killed* him.'

'I wasn't expecting him to entertain me,' Jenny replied. 'He's got about as much use for me as yesterday's suet pud. Tell me about Gwen,' she added. 'Was she his fiancée? A broken engagement may explain why Nigel keeps me at arm's length.'

'The least said about Gwen Ashcott the better,' Cynthia declared, giving vent to her feelings by banging the teapot on the table. 'She's a pain in the neck and I can't think why Nigel ever got engaged to her. She's not at all his type. She's rich and beautiful, but she's a spoilt little madam, and I pity the man she eventually leads to the altar. Between you and me and the gatepost I think Nigel's had a lucky escape. But it's going to take him a long time to recover. I wish he'd fall for a nice girl like you, Jenny, but I can't see it happening in a hurry.'

'I don't want him, thank you very much,' Jenny retorted.

'What a pity! He's the nicest man I know—barring Guy.'

'That's as may be, but his good points aren't very apparent at the moment.' Jenny dismissed the rare occasions when she had been privileged to witness the compassionate side to Nigel's nature. 'I suppose it's Gwen's fault, but he isn't exactly the life and soul of the party.'

'He hasn't got Alan's superficial charm, if that's what you're getting at,' Cynthia answered. 'But then—he never had. Neither has Guy, for that matter. But who wants candyfloss as a staple diet?' She hesitated. 'I hope you still haven't got a crush on Alan,' she said. 'Take my advice, Jenny, and steer clear of him. I hate to say this about my own brother but, as a long-term investment, he's a dead loss. We've seen so many of his girl friends come and go that we've lost count.'

Her warning was cut short by the appearance of Nigel, closely followed by Guy and, as they all sat down to the table, the talk became general, though Jenny was more silent than usual, and her glance strayed every now and then towards the empty chair. It was Alan she had come to see and, although she had enjoyed meeting up with Cynthia again, the visit had been slightly disappointing. 'Never mind,' she comforted herself, 'perhaps he'll phone me some time and make a date.'

She didn't really think he would, so she was pleasantly surprised when he got in touch with her a few days later. 'Hi!' he said over the phone. 'I thought you were supposed to be coming over to the farm to exercise Sweet Briar. How about this afternoon?'

This was typical of Alan. He had always been like it, expecting her to fall in with his plans at a moment's notice, but luckily she wasn't doing anything else, so she said one-thirty would suit her fine. He didn't offer to fetch her, probably assuming that she had her own car, so she would either have to walk or cycle, because the buses were too few and far between to be of much use.

She hadn't ridden her bicycle for ages, so it was horribly rusty and the tyres needed pumping up, but fortunately it was still roadworthy. She was wiping it over with an oily rag when Morwenna came into the garden to hang out some washing.

'Surely you aren't going to ride that old rattletrap?' she asked. 'I nearly chucked it out last spring when I was cleaning the garage.'

'I'm glad you didn't,' Jenny said. 'Bikes cost a bomb nowadays.'

'Well, I only hope the brakes are in good order. Where are you going?'

'To Wickhams' farm to exercise Cynthia's mare.' Jenny wasn't going to let on that she was meeting Alan again, but Morwenna wasn't deceived.

'I hope you know what you're doing,' she said. 'Alan Wickham's got a bad reputation where women are concerned.'

Jenny straightened up. 'Give a dog a bad name,' she retorted.

'That may be true,' Morwenna agreed, 'but there's no smoke without fire. Did you know he's been going around with Hilary Carfax?'

'What's wrong with that? She isn't married, is she?'

'No, but she broke off her engagement because of Alan. She was going to marry that nice boy, Colin Townsend, at Christmas and now it's all off. I think it's a shame, and it's not the first time it's happened. Before Hilary there was Emma Newport. *She* was engaged to Matthew Fussell but Alan threw a spanner in the works and, when he got tired of her, he dropped her like a hot brick. She's being treated now for depression.'

'I don't suppose it's all Alan's fault,' Jenny pointed out, wishing Morwenna would stop criticizing. 'He probably hasn't found the right girl.'

'And you hope it may be you?' Morwenna hung up several pairs of tights before she spoke again. 'Jenny, darling, do be careful,' she warned. 'I'm too fond of you to want you to be hurt.'

'Don't worry about me, Wenna,' Jenny replied. 'I'm old enough to take care of myself. Anyway, I'm sure Alan's not as black as he's painted.'

Morwenna didn't want to put Jenny's back up and she was wise enough to know when she had said enough. 'Well, he can't be much blacker than *you* at this very moment,' she laughed. 'Run along indoors and get cleaned up. Lunch is on the table and, if you don't get a move on, the best of the afternoon will be wasted.'

CHAPTER THREE

Jenny knew that Cynthia would be having her afternoon rest so, when she arrived at the farm, she went straight to the stable yard where she found Alan waiting for her. Dressed in a checked hacking jacket and riding breeches he looked handsomer than ever and she was dazzled by his good looks and charm.

'To think I've got Cousin Nigel to thank for bringing you into my life again,' he said, giving her a look which turned her knees to water. 'It's the first time he's ever done me a good turn.'

Some half-dozen horses were in their loose boxes and he paused momentarily in front of Baronet. 'Not today, old boy,' he said, and there was a note of regret in his voice. 'He's Guy's exclusive property,' he added by way of explanation. 'Nobody except his lordship is allowed to ride him.'

He had already saddled and bridled Sweet Briar and Jenny took some lumps of sugar out of the pocket of her jeans and fondled the mare while Alan led a bay gelding into the yard. She vaguely wondered why he had said 'not today, old boy', to Guy's horse. It almost sounded as if he rode Baronet on occasions when he was sure he wouldn't be found out, but she dismissed the idea as fanciful and soon forgot about it in the joy of cantering beside him across the downs.

They rode for the best part of an hour and her too-long disused muscles were beginning to ache when he drew rein and pointed with his riding crop to a huge oak standing sentinel on the skyline. 'Remember the kissing tree?' he asked. 'I'll race you to it.'

He had always been able to ride faster than she could and, by the time she caught up with him, he had dismounted and, with the reins looped over one arm, he was studying the initials cut into the trunk by generations of young lovers. 'It's like looking for a needle in a haystack,' he said, and he directed a laughing glance at her from under his long lashes. 'See if you can find our mark before I can.'

She pointed unhesitatingly to a spot just above eye-level where, surrounded by a roughly drawn heart and pierced by an arrow, the initials J and A still showed clearly despite the passage of time. 'That takes us back a bit, doesn't it?' he remarked. 'It must have been six or seven years ago, when we were just a couple of kids. But they were good times, weren't they, Jenny?'

'Yes,' she agreed. 'We had a lot of fun together. Riding, fishing, swimming . . .'

'And making love?' he prompted.

Her face flamed. 'Alan—we *didn't*! You hardly ever even kissed me. We were only children.'

Remembering those kisses . . . the sweet, exploratory kisses of an innocent boy and girl, she was seized with a sudden shyness and, without waiting for Alan to remount, she pulled on Sweet Briar's reins and urged the mare to a canter. She didn't stop to analyse her behaviour. She only knew she wanted to put as much distance as possible between herself and the kissing tree.

He caught up with her far too quickly for her peace of mind, but he made no comment, merely contenting himself with an amused glance which she pretended not to notice. 'We'll go that-away,' he said, pointing to the main road and presently they came within sight of a large house standing in its own grounds and set well back from the road. A small lodge stood beside the heavy wrought-iron gates but there was nobody about and, to Jenny's surprise, Alan dismounted and, pushing open the gates, he waited for her to follow him.

'It's private property,' she protested. 'Are you sure it's all right for us to go in?'

'The Ashcotts are in Canada, visiting relatives,' he answered. 'I often come here. I like to pretend I'm lord of the manor.' He gave her a sidelong, laughing glance. 'Come on, Jenny. Don't be such a spoil sport.'

'Oh—all right,' she agreed, rather unwillingly, 'but only on condition that you take the blame if we're caught.'

'No fear of that,' he grinned. 'In any case, I know the caretakers and they don't mind me trespassing.'

Feeling slightly less apprehensive Jenny urged Sweet Briar forward and waited until Alan caught up with her. 'Did you say the Ashcotts live here?' she asked. 'Wasn't Nigel engaged to Gwen Ashcott at one time?'

Alan nodded. 'I can't think why he was such an idiot as to break it off. A girl like that, with beauty, brains and a sizeable bank account. He must have been mad.'

'What happened?' Jenny asked. Cynthia hadn't told her the ins and outs of the affair and she was intensely interested to hear all the details. 'Why was the engagement broken off?'

Alan shrugged. 'Your guess is as good as mine,' he answered. 'Nigel wasn't exactly forthcoming but, putting two and two together, I'd say Gwen went a bit too far. She wanted to have her cake and eat it. To put it more bluntly she had no intention of curbing her natural instincts just because she was wearing Nigel's ring.'

'I don't see the point of her getting engaged to him if she didn't love him,' Jenny argued.

'I imagine she wanted a respectable marriage. There was something of a scandal when she had an affair with a gipsy a year or two ago and no doubt there were other indiscretions. Nigel should have turned a blind eye. She would probably have settled down to being quite a good wife in the long run.'

The drive was bordered with lime trees, and the fallen leaves lay in a thick carpet through which the horses' hooves shuffled, making a sound like a series of pistol shots. The house itself was barred and shuttered, but the garden was in good order, with the grass cut and the edges neatly clipped. Also the rose trees had been pruned and the flower beds tidied, so, even though the place was unlived in, there was no sign of neglect.

'When are the Ashcotts coming back from Canada?' Jenny asked.

'Soon after Christmas, I believe. Mr Ashcott died a few months ago and Gwen thought a holiday abroad would do her mother good, though personally I think it was Gwen who wanted to get away. There was a lot of unpleasant gossip when the engagement was broken off.'

'If Nigel's still here when they return perhaps there'll be a reconciliation,' Jenny suggested.

Alan laughed. 'I can't see my cousin climbing down from his high horse,' he said. 'I imagine he'll bend over backwards to avoid a meeting.'

'That may be difficult,' Jenny pointed out. 'I believe Mrs Ashcott is a patient of Doctor Hatherley's and the time may come when Nigel has to call at the manor to see her. Doctor Hatherley hasn't been at all well lately and, with the winter coming on, he'll often be housebound.'

'Could be an embarrassing situation,' Alan remarked in an amused voice. 'If I was in Nigel's shoes I'd swallow my pride and try and make a go of it—being the lord of the manor could be a pretty enviable position.' By now they had reached the end of the drive and, as their horses clip-clopped across the wide forecourt, he waved his hand in a proprietorial gesture. 'What do you think of the place?' he asked. 'It's not a bad little shanty, is it?'

Although he spoke lightly she thought she could detect a note of envy in his voice, and this was hardly surprising because the house was extremely beautiful. She stared at it in open admiration: the flight of shallow steps leading to the brass-studded front door: the elegant archway on the left through which could be glimpsed a courtyard and outbuildings.

But the fact that they were trespassing spoilt her pleasure. 'I'm sure we shouldn't be here,' she said, but he merely laughed.

'I've already told you I know the caretakers,' he reminded her. 'Matter of fact I'm Ma Pike's blue-eyed boy.'

'Do they live at the lodge?' she asked, remembering the pretty little house standing beside the wrought iron gates.

'That's right. There's Ma and Pa Pike and their daughter Shirley. Quite a little happy family. Pa does the garden and Ma sees to the house.'

'How old is Shirley?' Jenny asked, only idly curious. 'Is she a little girl or is she grown up?'

His lips twitched with amusement. 'I'd say she's very grown up,' he answered. 'She works at the new paint factory so she earns good wages and, by the look of her, I'd say she spends all the money on herself. You might call her the local Marilyn Monroe—at any rate, all the boys are round her like bees round a honey pot.'

Something in the way he spoke gave Jenny the uncomfortable feeling that he, too, found Shirley attractive, but commonsense told her it was hardly likely that a man in Alan's position would take much notice of a caretaker's daughter. 'I think we ought to go,' she said. 'I'm supposed to be exercising Sweet Briar, not doing a tour of the stately homes of England.'

'Please stay a bit longer,' he pleaded. 'Now we've come as far as this you might as well see everything.'

'Oh—all right,' she agreed, and she followed him rather reluctantly through the archway. When they had tethered the horses they strolled round the garden and she admired the well-kept lawn with its sundial and cedar tree. Presently they came to the tennis court and swimming-pool and, beyond again, were acres of beautiful parkland. 'It's huge, isn't it!' she exclaimed.

'Yes,' he agreed. 'The Ashcotts are stinking rich.' He pointed to a handsome, stone-built house half-hidden by a belt of trees. 'That's where the estate manager lives,' he continued. 'If you ask me, old Buckleigh has a cushy job. I wouldn't sneeze at it myself.'

She pulled on his arm, again conscious of a feeling of unease. 'He's probably watching us,' she said. 'We ought to hurry or I'll be cycling home in the dark.'

'I'll drive you back,' he offered. 'Your cycle can go on the roof rack. I want to show you the inside of the manor before we go.'

She shot him a startled glance. 'You can't get in,' she protested. 'The whole place is shut up.'

He told her one of the side windows was unfastened and that it was easy to effect an entry. 'If you'll wait for me at the back door I'll let you in,' he said. 'I won't be more than a few minutes.'

Knowing he would be annoyed with her if she raised any further objections she allowed herself to be persuaded, but she found herself looking guiltily over her shoulder, fearful that Mr Buckleigh might appear and angrily order her off the premises.

Alan led her through the servants' quarters to the front of the house, and she stood beside him in the enormous hall and stared in silence at the beautiful curved staircase which led up to a picture gallery. 'This is where the New Year's Eve ball is held,' he said and he swept her into his arms and laughingly waltzed round the room with her. 'Can you imagine the scene?' he asked. 'The girls in their lovely gowns and the men in full evening dress. It could be us. Lady Jennifer Clayton and Sir Alan Wickham.'

For a moment Jenny entered into his game of 'let's pretend'. She could hear the strains of music from an imaginary orchestra, she could see the couples dancing in the old-fashioned way, with their arms around each other, and, with a sigh of content, she closed her eyes and wished the make-believe could last for ever.

Presently they came to a standstill, breathless and laughing but, instead of releasing her, his arms tightened round her waist and his mouth came down on hers in a kiss that was very much more adult than the ones they had exchanged years ago under the kissing tree. In more favourable circumstances she might have responded with the same ardour but dusk was falling and there was now very little light left in the ballroom. The fact that they had no right to be in the house aggravated her feeling of panic and she pulled herself out of his demanding arms and insisted that it was time to go.

'Just as you like,' he said, with a sudden change of mood, and his tone was nicely calculated to show what he thought of her behaviour. 'It would never do to keep you out after dark.'

'Don't be like that, Alan,' she pleaded, almost having to run to keep pace with him as he strode towards the servants' quarters. 'I've got to get back in time for evening surgery.'

'Oh, well—if that's the only reason for your old maidish behaviour we'll forget about it,' he said on a slightly more friendly note, and she was thankful she had been able to think of a legitimate excuse for leaving so hurriedly.

Mounting their horses they rode in silence down the drive and, just as they reached the gates, a bus drew up and an exceptionally pretty girl alighted. She was carrying a large cardboard dress-box and quite evidently she was returning home from a shopping expedition.

Alan looked momentarily taken aback when she waved to him but he passed off the situation with his usual aplomb. 'Marilyn Monroe in person,' he whispered to Jenny. 'Hi, Shirley—how come you've got the afternoon off?'

'Had some shopping to do,' she answered airily. 'I came over giddy this morning and they sent me home.'

'You'll "come over giddy" once too often,' he warned, knowing full well she was continually taking time off on one pretext or another. 'Aren't you afraid of getting the sack?'

She grinned. 'I've got friends in high places,' she boasted, and he laughed, condoning her behaviour because she was pretty and could get away with it.

'Open the gates, there's a good girl,' he said. 'We're in rather a hurry.'

'Yes, your honour.' Shirley giggled, dropping him a curtsy and, although she did as she was told, she made it abundantly clear she wasn't taking orders from him.

The exchanges puzzled Jenny who hadn't been blind to the scowl which was directed at her when Alan wasn't looking. For no reason that she could understand she was this girl's enemy, and she found the whole set-up vaguely disturbing. It almost seemed as if Shirley had a hold over Alan, and Jenny shied away from the rather sordid implications.

Whatever it was, she didn't want to know.

'I won't stop to see Cynthia,' she said when they arrived back at the farm, 'but tell her I'll come along again in a day or two.'

'The sooner the better,' he answered. 'Sweet Briar needs regular exercise and perhaps you won't be in such a hurry next time.' The remark could be taken in two ways and she flushed as she met his meaningful glance. At any rate he appeared to have recovered his good humour and she guessed he had an easy-going temperament and that he would never remain out of sorts for very long.

'Honestly there's no need to drive me home,' she said when they had rubbed down the horses. 'It won't take me more than fifteen minutes on my bike.'

'Except that you haven't got any lights,' he pointed out.

Crestfallen she followed him to the car and he tossed her bicycle onto the roof rack in one easy movement. 'How stupid of me,' she said. 'Actually I haven't ridden a bike for ages and I never thought about lights. In any case I didn't expect to be out for such a long time, and I'd forgotten it gets dark so early now that we've changed the clocks.'

She knew she was babbling like an idiot and the amused expression on his face made her feel more uncomfortable than ever. 'Pipe down, Jenny,' he laughed, 'or I shall begin to think you engineered it on purpose so that I'd have to drive you home.'

This was so nearly the truth that she felt herself blushing and she was glad the fast-gathering darkness hid her discomfiture. According to Cynthia, Alan's conquests were so easily accomplished he didn't value them, and the last thing Jenny wanted was for him to suspect she was chasing him.

She thought he would just drop her at the front door but he seemed to expect to be invited in to meet Richard and Morwenna, so she did so, rather unwillingly, and she left them talking while she disappeared to have a quick bath. When she came downstairs again her heart sank because he was chatting up Carol, who had returned earlier than expected from having tea with a friend. Although she was still judged not to be fit enough to go back to college, Jenny had been encouraging her to pick up the threads of her social life, and she was quite happy to visit her friends as long as she was fetched and brought back by car.

Now that she had more appetite she was putting on a little weight and, although she was still very thin, she had lost the transparent look which had been so frightening. Looking at her now, 'Nurse' Jenny was proud of the progress her patient had made during the past few weeks. On the other hand 'sister' Jenny had mixed feelings, because Carol was a born flirt and she was certainly giving Alan the full treatment.

In an effort not to show how browned off she was with her sister for butting in on her territory, she cut her good-byes short. 'I'll be off now,' she said casually. 'Thanks for the lift, Alan. Be seeing you.'

'Wait a minute,' he protested. 'Where do you think you're going in such a hurry? I'll give you a lift to the surgery.' He downed his drink and followed her out of the door. 'Wow! Your sister!' he exclaimed. 'She's another Shirley Pike.'

Jenny wondered what Carol's reaction would be if she knew she was being likened to the local Marilyn Monroe. It was certainly an apt comparison because they were both exceptionally pretty and neither of them had any scruples about using their charms to get what they wanted. 'I'm afraid I can't compete with Carol,' she said, trying to make a joke of it. 'She always pinches my boy friends.'

'Is that a fact? Well, here's one boy friend she won't be pinching,' he assured her, and he gave her a careless hug. 'Be seeing you,' he said. 'Sweet Briar needs exercising every day so don't leave it too long before you come again.'

She was five minutes late for surgery and, as she entered the house, she thanked her lucky stars it was Doctor Hatherley and not Doctor Barrett who was on duty. But it seemed that her luck had run out. She was hastily donning her overall when the consulting-room door burst open and Nigel stormed out. 'Miss Clayton!' he exploded. 'And about time, too! I've got a patient waiting whose case history has gone missing. Kindly find it for me. Miss Meade. Miss Margaret Meade. It should be in the files under the letter M,' he added scathingly.

'I'm sorry, Doctor Barrett.' Jenny thought it would be tactful to apologize although, in point of fact, she was not to blame. Miss Meade was a new patient and, owing to a postal error, her case history had not yet been passed on by her previous doctor. Jenny pointed this out to Nigel but her explanation did little to soften his annoyance.

'If you'd turned up at the proper time I wouldn't have had to waste precious minutes looking for non-existent papers,' he remarked in tones of icy politeness, and he turned on his heel and went back to the consulting-room, leaving Jenny to ponder miserably about his unfair attitude.

'I wish he was more like his cousin,' she thought. 'I don't seem able to do anything to please him, however hard I try.'

But later that evening, after the last patient had departed, she was tidying the waiting-room when he put his head round the door. 'I'm sorry I was so abrupt with you,' he said, rather less brusquely than usual, 'but I didn't expect to have to take surgery this evening.'

'Surprise, surprise!' Jenny thought. 'An

apology from his lordship. Whatever's come over him?'

'That's all right,' she answered. 'It was a pretty hectic evening and I don't blame you for losing your cool. What happened to Doctor Hatherley?'

'He had an urgent phone call from the hospital, notifying him that one of his patients was dying, so he asked me to take over at the last minute.'

'Not Mrs Cottrell?' Jenny asked anxiously. Violet Cottrell was a widow with five children and, since she was taken ill several months ago, her eighteen-year-old daughter had been trying to cope, but things weren't at all easy. They lived in an isolated cottage and, beside herself and her sixteen-year-old brother, there was a ten-year-old girl who had a weak chest, a toddler and a young baby. 'Whatever will Doris do? I suppose the little ones will be taken into care.'

'I don't see why. Doris strikes me as being a capable young woman and she should be able to manage, particularly if the neighbours rally round.'

'Neighbours? Do you realize where the Cottrells live? It's the other end of nowhere.'

'Of course I know where they live,' he answered impatiently. 'I admit it's a bit isolated but I doubt if it's more than half a mile from the Wickhams. In my opinion, whatever the difficulties, the family should stick together.'

There was a doubtful look on Jenny's face. 'I'm afraid the authorities will intervene,' she said.

'Then they'll have me to reckon with,' Nigel declared, 'and I'm sure I shall have Doctor Hatherley's full support.' The determined expression on his face boded ill for any bureaucrat who dared to argue with him.

'If there's anything I can do,' Jenny offered. 'Would it help if I went to see Doris? I don't want to butt in where I'm not wanted, but she's bound to have lots of problems and I don't suppose the health visitor will call very often.'

'That sounds to me like a good idea,' Nigel spoke approvingly. 'You could keep an eye on the little girl. The rest of the family seem healthy enough but Linda has a weak chest and she's had one attack of bronchitis already this autumn. It strikes me that the cottage is cold and damp and not the right sort of place for a delicate child.'

There was a note of very real concern in his voice, and Jenny found herself warming towards him. Why couldn't he always be like this, ready and willing to discuss the welfare of his patients with her? Instead he was often taciturn and even, on occasions, downright rude.

'I'd better not go and see them until after the funeral,' she decided. 'It's possible one of their relatives will offer them a home.'

'I can't see even the most caring of relatives throwing open their doors to a family of five children,' he pointed out. 'They might take the two youngest but I'm sure Doris wouldn't be parted from them. There's another problem too. The eldest boy is a bit of a tearaway and he's already been in trouble with the police. Now that he's left school Guy has given him a job on the farm and he seems to be making a go of it, but a move might prove disastrous. Taking everything into consideration, I would say it's essential for the Cottrells to stay together as a family unit.'

'Life's not a bit fair,' Jenny burst out. 'It's a shame how some families are dogged by ill-fortune while others go scot free. First Sam Cottrell dying and then his wife. They say everything goes in threes, and Doris must be wondering where fate will strike next. It could be Linda.'

Nigel raised an eyebrow. 'Superstitious nonsense,' he declared. 'But I do agree with you about the less deserving cases going scot free. I see red every time I deal with the malingerers who take advantage of Doctor Hatherley's good nature. This evening, for instance. There were at least three patients who ought to have been signed off a week ago.'

Jenny giggled. 'They must have had a nasty shock when they discovered you were on duty instead of Doctor Hatherley.'

'They were not the only ones to have a nasty shock,' Nigel remarked meaningly, and, with this sly dig in her direction, he turned on his heel and left her staring after him open-mouthed. Was it possible that, under his stuffed shirt, Doctor Barrett possessed a sense of humour after all?

The following Saturday Alan phoned Jenny to ask why she hadn't been to the farm again to exercise Sweet Briar. 'Do come today,' he coaxed. 'I plan to ride in any case but it will be much more enjoyable if you can come too.'

Cynthia had warned her not to listen to her brother's blarney but, when he used that particular tone of voice, Jenny was powerless to resist. 'All right,' she agreed. 'I'll be along about one-thirty, same as last time.'

When she arrived at the farm Alan had already saddled Sweet Briar but his own mount was nowhere to be seen. 'Pineapple Lad's gone lame,' he explained, 'so I'll have to make do with a substitute.'

He went back to the loose boxes and she wasn't at all surprised when he led out the big chestnut stallion. 'I thought you said Guy didn't allow you to ride Baronet,' she remarked.

Alan winked. 'What the eye doesn't see,' he replied. 'Guy's gone to a meeting and he won't be back till late tonight.'

It seemed a rather deceitful way to behave but an argument wouldn't be a very good start to the afternoon, so Jenny bit her lip and remained silent. She salved her conscience by telling herself it was extremely selfish of Guy to refuse to let his brother-in-law ride his horse. It wasn't as if Alan was a careless rider. He rode with ease and assurance and it was surely better for Baronet to be exercised rather than spend the afternoon cooped up in the stables.

Sensing her disapproval Alan turned on all his charm and he was such a pleasant companion she soon forgot her nagging doubts. Even the weather conspired to make it a memorable afternoon and it was difficult to believe it was already November, for the air was mild and the sky a cloudless blue. Autumn had lingered longer than usual and, in the more sheltered spots, the heather was still purple, and clumps of yellow gorse scented the air with musk.

Presently they reined in their horses and looked across the valley to where the azure sea shimmered in the far distance. 'Let's stretch our legs,' Alan suggested and, without waiting for an answer, he dismounted and tethered Baronet to a rocky outcrop. Jenny hesitated. On horseback she was safe but, if she followed suit, she wasn't sure how Alan would behave. His recent kiss was still vivid in her mind and she wasn't yet ready for a repeat performance.

Almost as if he could read her thoughts he gave her a sidelong glance and his lips twitched with amusement. 'I'll behave,' he promised. 'Cross my heart and hope to die. In any event you're well chaperoned.' He indicated a lone sheep who had become separated from her sisters, and who was regarding them with a supercilious stare.

Jenny laughed. 'In that case I'll risk it,' she said and, ignoring his proffered hand, she dismounted and tethered Sweet Briar some distance away from Baronet.

Alan fell into step beside her. 'I can't imagine why I didn't recognize you the other day when you came to the farm with Nigel,' he said. 'You haven't altered all that much from when you were a schoolgirl.'

Jenny frowned. 'Meaning I still behave like a child?' she asked. 'That's not a very nice thing to say.'

'I meant it as a compliment,' he replied, rather too glibly. 'You've kept an air of old-fashioned innocence, like the bloom on a grape. Most girls lose it when they grow up, more's the pity.'

It was a pretty speech but Jenny wasn't deceived by it. 'Thanks very much,' she said stormily. 'Just because I didn't respond to your advances quite as enthusiastically as you expected, you seem to think I'm retarded.'

He backed away from her in mock alarm. 'Don't bite my head off, Jenny,' he pleaded. 'I apologize for my behaviour. I was a moron and a clot and I grovel at your feet. Please say you forgive me.'

It was impossible to remain angry with him for long and, peace being restored, they resumed their interrupted walk and came presently to a small stream, so shallow it was possible to cross it by stepping stones.

'I'm not going to get my feet wet,' Alan declared, and he rolled up his denims and took off his socks and shoes. Jenny followed him across and, when they got to the other side, they looked at each other and laughed.

'Why did we bother to come?' Jenny asked. 'We've only got to cross back again to fetch the horses.'

Alan curled his toes under. 'My feet are freezing,' he declared. 'Let's get it over with as quickly as possible.'

He clowned across on tiptoe, with Jenny following close behind him, and she was laughing so much at his antics she slipped on the last stone and fell into the water. Wet to the waist she grabbed his outstretched hand and floundered onto the bank like a hooked fish.

'I'm simply sopping,' she grumbled.

'You'd better strip off and put on my sweater or you'll freeze to death,' he said and, tactfully turning his back on her, he waited while she carried out his instructions.

'Thank you,' she said in a small voice when she was ready, and he turned round and surveyed her with a bold tenderness which she found disconcerting.

'What a compromising situation,' he remarked. 'And our chaperone is nowhere to be seen.'

Jenny's eyes flashed. 'You promised to behave,' she reminded him, and she snatched up her wet clothes and marched off in the direction of the tethered horses.

When they got back to the farm Alan volunteered to rub down the horses while Jenny went indoors to borrow some dry clothes from Cynthia, who rolled her eyes heavenwards when she heard what had happened. 'I wouldn't be surprised if Alan did it on purpose,' she declared. 'He really is the limit. You'd better go and have a hot bath, Jenny—your legs are positively blue with cold.'

She came into the bathroom with a change of clothing while Jenny was still soaking in the bath and she suggested that, as there was no surgery on Saturday evening, she might like to stay to supper. 'I shall be all alone,' she added persuasively. 'Guy won't be back till late and I'm sure he'll give you a lift home.'

'That would be nice,' Jenny replied, 'but Alan said he might take me out for a meal.'

Cynthia frowned. 'I thought he was already going out,' she said.

'Well, he did say something about a date but he said it wasn't important and he could easily cry off.'

'That's typical of Alan,' Cynthia remarked.

'Look, Jenny, I don't want to interfere but, for goodness sake, don't get too fond of him. Wherever he goes he leaves a trail of broken hearts behind him.'

'Perhaps he's searching for the right girl,' Jenny suggested. 'It could be me.'

'Well, watch your step, young lady. Alan's like a spoilt child. He's always hankering after something new and, when he's got it, he doesn't value it.'

And, on this warning note, she went out of the bathroom, leaving a subdued Jenny to mull over what she had said.

Going downstairs some ten minutes later Jenny overheard the tail end of an argument going on between brother and sister, and she hesitated outside the kitchen door, not really meaning to listen but not liking to interrupt.

'I call it a disgraceful way to behave,' Cynthia was saying in a furious voice. 'You promised Hilary you'd take her to the dance tonight and you can't possibly stand her up at the last moment.'

'I don't see why I should go if I don't want to,' Alan answered rather sulkily. 'I'm sick and tired of the way she can't leave me alone. Always ringing me up and shooting her mouth if I don't pay court to her morning, noon and night.'

'That's not fair,' Cynthia protested. 'You were the one who made a dead set at her, and you weren't satisfied until she broke off with that nice Colin Townsend she'd been going with before you came on the scene. I warn you, Alan, if you ring her up with some rotten excuse about not being able to take her to the dance, I'll spill the beans to Jenny. You needn't ask Hilary out again if you don't want to, but for heaven's sake have the decency to let her down gently.'

'Okay, okay,' he grumbled. 'I'll behave like a proper little gentleman if you insist. But mind you don't sneak off and tell Jenny. She's rather special and I don't want anything to spoil our relationship.'

'All your girls are special to begin with,' Cynthia retorted. 'If you break Jenny's heart I'll never forgive you.'

Jenny didn't want Alan to know she had overheard this conversation, so she tiptoed back along the passage and, when he came out of the kitchen, she was apparently just coming downstairs. 'Thanks for the loan of your sweater,' she said. 'It probably saved my life.'

He put his hand on the banisters and, when she reached the bottom stair, he barred her way and stood looking at her in a way that caused her heart to beat faster. She knew she was being foolish to succumb so easily to his charm but she couldn't help herself. She forgot Cynthia's warning words, she forgot the quarrel she had just overheard and the disturbing reference to past and present girl friends. Instead she remembered only what she wanted to remember. 'Jenny is special,' he had said, and she rejoiced to know that her feelings were reciprocated.

He was just about to kiss her when the kitchen door opened and Cynthia came along the passage. 'Oh, there you are, Jenny!' she exclaimed. 'Alan's just been telling me he can't very well get out of his date this evening, so do stay and have supper with me. Would you like to phone your stepmother and let her know Guy will drive you home later this evening?'

'Sorry about that, Jenny,' Alan said in a flat voice. 'Perhaps another time?'

'I'll look forward to it,' she answered and, pretending not to see the scowl that passed between brother and sister, she picked up the phonc and dialled her home number.

Alan left about seven and Jenny and Cynthia spent a cosy evening by the fire, talking about their schooldays and looking at old snapshots. Guy didn't get back till after eleven and Jenny was glad she had stayed because Cynthia was beginning to get fidgety and, being a nurse, she knew that any emotional upset would be bad for her friend in her present condition.

'It was nice of you to keep Cynthia company,' Guy remarked as he drove her home. 'I don't like leaving her on her own in the evenings, particularly since her last miscarriage, but sometimes it's unavoidable, like tonight when I was chairing a meeting.'

'No, she shouldn't be left alone in the house after dark,' Jenny agreed. 'Let me know next time you've got to be out late and I'll be glad to keep her company.'

'Thanks, Jenny. I'm more than grateful. She had a bad haemorrhage last time and we're both scared stiff of it happening again.' He broke off and gave her a rather embarrassed smile. 'I hope you won't think we're making use of you,' he continued. 'Exercising Sweet Briar and keeping an eye on Cynthia will keep you busy and I know you don't get much spare time.'

'I'm fond of Cynthia and it's no hardship to exercise Sweet Briar,' she answered. 'In fact I count myself lucky. Most people have to pay through the nose to hire a horse and go riding but I get it all for free. It was gorgeous on the downs today, blue sky and sunshine and almost like midsummer. If it hadn't been for exercising Sweet Briar I would have probably spent the afternoon cooped up indoors.'

'Did Alan go with you?' Guy asked. 'Yes, I thought so. As a matter of interest which horse did he ride?' Seeing Jenny hesitate, his mouth tightened. 'You needn't answer,' he said. 'It was hardly a fair question.'

'Alan's a good rider,' Jenny remarked. 'Why do you object to him exercising Baronet?'

'Because Baronet happens to be my horse. Alan has ridden him several times without my permission. Once he let him dry off without rubbing him down and, on another occasion, Baronet cast a shoe and went lame and Alan didn't bother to tell me. As a result I couldn't ride in the point-to-point the following Saturday.' He stopped the car outside Jenny's gate and left the engine ticking over while she got out. 'Thanks for everything,' he said. 'See you again in a day or two.'

'Who brought you home?' Carol asked as Jenny came through the front door. 'He made a pretty quick getaway whoever he was.'

'It was Guy Morris, Cynthia's husband,' Jenny answered, ignoring the innuendo behind her sister's words. 'Didn't Morwenna tell you he was giving me a lift home?'

'No, she didn't mention it. Actually, I thought you were going out with Alan tonight. What happened? Did he ditch you for another girl?'

'I didn't say I was definitely going out with Alan,' Jenny answered, wishing that Carol hadn't listened so avidly to her telephone conversation earlier in the day. 'If you really want to know, I spent the evening with Cynthia.'

'What a bore!' Carol gave an exaggerated yawn. 'Never mind, darling. Better luck next time.'

CHAPTER FOUR

Jenny wasn't altogether sure whether or not she wanted there to be a next time. It was quite on the cards that Alan would treat her just as badly as he had apparently treated his other girl friends but, although her common-sense told her it would be wiser not to encourage him, her heart wouldn't listen and, when he phoned her at the surgery on Monday morning, to ask her to go out with him that evening, she had no hesitation in accepting his invitation.

He picked her up at eight o'clock and they called in at a pub to have a drink. Some of Alan's friends were there: a rowdy lot who Jenny didn't care for, and she was relieved, though somewhat surprised, when he didn't linger.

'Where would you like to go for a meal?' he asked, when they got back to the car, and she said she would leave the choice to him.

'Nothing too fancy,' she stipulated. 'I'm so hungry I could eat a horse, and in any case I'm not dressed for high society.'

'Then I vote we go back to the farm,' he said casually.

Jenny thought this was a bit of a come-down. She had been looking forward to spending the evening alone with Alan but, apparently, he was quite happy for it to be a family party. 'I don't think that's a very good idea,' she objected. 'Cynthia won't be best pleased at having to provide a meal when she was expecting you to be out.'

Alan grinned. 'As a matter of fact she and Guy won't be there. It's their wedding anniversary and they've gone out to celebrate. It'll be just the two of us, Jenny. Meat pie and pickled onions. Apple tart and cream. As much bread and cheese as you can eat. And I've got a bottle of bubbly in the back of the car.'

She knew Alan well enough to guess this was what he had been planning all along. 'Just the two of us'. The words spelt out a promise but they also spelt out danger, and Jenny was torn two ways. 'I'm not sure . . .' she began hesitantly.

'Darling, grow up,' Alan pleaded, and his ardent look turned Jenny's knees to water.

'Okay,' she said. 'If you insist. I really am terribly hungry and meat pie and pickles sound fabulous.'

Well satisfied with the success of his plans, Alan got into the car beside her and drove fast and recklessly along the main road until they came to the turning leading to the farm. He had to slow down then, because the track was muddy but, even so, they reached their destination far too quickly for Jenny's peace of mind. What was she letting herself in for, she wondered. And, for two pins, she would have asked him to turn around and drive her back to the comparative safety of a public eating place.

They ate their supper in the warm kitchen and, after they had cleared away the dishes and washed up, they took their coffee into the living-room. Alan had built up the fire as soon as they came in, and the flames were leaping up the chimney and casting such a rosy glow that further light was unnecessary.

Alan took his ease in the comfortable old armchair which had belonged to his father, while Jenny sat opposite him in the small upright chair where Mrs Wickham used to sit during the long winter evenings, darning socks or doing the mending. 'What a cosy domestic scene,' Alan remarked. 'What more could a man wish for than to sit by his own fireside with his chosen companion.' His serious manner was in marked contrast to his usual flippancy and Jenny wondered what was coming next. 'This is *my* home, Jenny,' he continued, 'but when Cynthia and Guy are here I feel like an intruder. I sometimes wonder what will happen when I get married. Will my wife be content to share the house with my sister and brother-in-law?'

'Would that be necessary?' Jenny asked. 'Surely Cynthia and Guy would move out and buy another house for themselves. After all, you're the only son and I presume the farm belongs to *you*, and that your sister and her husband are only living here by grace of favour.'

Alan's brow darkened. 'That's what is so grossly unfair,' he remarked. 'By all rights the farm should be mine, but Dad and I had an almighty bust up a few years ago and when he died he left everything to Cynthia. I'm the one who's living here by grace of favour and, I tell you frankly, it makes my blood boil to have to play second fiddle to Guy. Just because he married Cynthia he's had everything handed to him on a plate.'

'Yes, that does seem unfair,' Jenny agreed, 'but surely Cynthia would have the decency to make a generous contribution if you decided to move out and buy a house of your own? Alternatively she might have no objection to sharing her home with another woman, especially if she was fond of her.'

'Two she-cats in one kitchen?' Alan gave a short laugh. 'That wouldn't suit Cynthia at all. As for making a contribution towards my expenses—well, that's a laugh. My darling sister has always kept a tight hold of the purse strings and I'm never around when she dispenses charity. So you see, my sweet Jenny, I'm out on a limb. What I really want is a farm of my own. A place where I can be my own master. Pie in the sky as far as I'm concerned. Farms cost a small fortune nowadays and, if I left Wickhams', the best I could hope for would be a farm managership, which wouldn't suit me at all. My other alternative would be to apply for an estate managership. I've got my eye on Frank Buckleigh's job and he's due to retire next year.'

'He's the Ashcotts' estate manager, isn't he?'

'Yes—I showed you his house the other day. It's a nice place and it goes with the job. How does the idea of living there appeal to you?'

Jenny's heart began to race but she forced herself to give a flippant answer. 'Whatever are you suggesting?' she asked. 'You can't be asking me to *marry* you at this early stage of our acquaintance.'

'Well, no, not exactly. I'm putting out a few feelers, that's all. But it's not as if we've only just met. Remember the old days? The times we spent together? The kissing tree?'

'Yes, but we were only children.' Jenny's laugh was unsteady. 'We've changed a lot since then.'

'We've grown up, if that's what you mean. And so much the better.' His voice thickened and, with one lithe movement, he got to his feet and stood looking down at her, matching his will against hers. 'Jenny,' he said softly. 'Darling Jenny, I want you.'

The next moment she was in his arms, with no awareness of how she got there and, before she knew what was happening, he was kissing her long and passionately, with an expertise against which she had no defence. Afterwards she wondered what would have happened if they hadn't been disturbed by a peremptory knocking at the door.

'Mr Wickham, sir. Mr Wickham.' It was one of the farm hands to say a cow was having difficulty calving and would Alan phone the vet straightaway.

The love scene was well and truly over. Abruptly Alan let Jenny go and, with a muttered oath, he marched angrily into the hall to dial the vet's number. When he returned Jenny had already fetched her coat and was waiting for him to take her home. 'I'm sorry, Jenny,' he said ruefully. 'What a way for the evening to end.'

He looked so put out that Jenny began to laugh. 'Saved by the bell from a fate worse than death,' she giggled and, after a moment, Alan saw the funny side.

'You're a good sport, Jenny,' he said, and he pulled her into his arms for one last kiss but, this time, she was ready for him, and she hastily turned her face away so that only her cheek was visible.

'Not again, Alan—please,' she said breathlessly.

'Perhaps you're right,' he agreed. He could afford to play a waiting game because he knew she wouldn't be able to hold out against him indefinitely. The sweetness of her response had made it very clear that she was in love with him, and it was now only a matter of time before he could add her name to his long list of conquests. 'Guy and Cynthia may get back early so we'd better call it a day.'

One last caress before he released her and then they went out to the car and, for the whole journey home, they only exchanged small-talk. Jenny was glad of this because it left her free to mull over what had happened between them. In many ways it had been a wonderful evening, but she wasn't too happy about the set-up. It had been dishonest of Alan to take advantage of Cynthia's and Guy's absence, just as it had been dishonest of him to visit the manor when its owners were abroad and, if she wasn't careful, he would tempt her into further wrong-doing. Marriage had been tentatively suggested but only in the far distant future, and she suspected it was like a carrot being dangled in front of the donkey's nose—the donkey, in this case, being herself.

Jenny sighed. She should have been over the moon with joy but, instead, she felt out of sorts and depressed. 'It's a pity you can't be vaccinated against falling in love,' she thought. 'It's a disease, like measles and whooping cough, and it should be avoided at all costs.'

And yet . . . and yet . . . The memory of Alan's lips on hers sent her smiling to sleep and he walked with her in her dreams, so that, when she woke next morning, her first thought was of when she would see him again. Today?

Tomorrow? The next day? But, as it turned out, it was nearly three weeks before their next meeting and during that period she had plenty of time to have second thoughts.

* * *

A week after Mrs Cottrell's funeral she cycled over to the cottage to see how Doris was getting on. Morwenna had given her some home-made plum jam and a batch of cakes to take with her and she had bought a few toys for the little ones and a book for Linda, but she didn't want it to be thought she was dispensing charity, so she decided to wait and see how the land lay before offering her gifts.

Leaving her bicycle propped against the gate she walked up the path and rang the front door bell. There was no answer so she went round to the back of the house and found Doris busily engaged in digging the vegetable patch. The toddler was filling a bucket with discarded stones and the baby was sitting up in his pram, placidly sucking his thumb.

Doris gave her an unfriendly look. 'You'll be Miss Clayton,' she said, almost rudely. 'You needn't have bothered yourself with calling. Didn't Doctor Barrett tell you we're managing fine on our own?'

'Yes, he did,' Jenny answered, rather put off by the unenthusiastic greeting, 'but I thought I'd come all the same. Just in case you're needing anything.'

'Like what?' came the quick retort. 'We're not in need of charity, if that's what you're getting at.'

Jenny was thankful she had left her gifts in the saddle bag. 'I wouldn't dream of offering you charity,' she said. 'This is just a friendly call to see if I can help in any way. I'm sorry about your mother,' she added impulsively. 'I know how much you must miss her.'

Doris bit her lip and turned away to hide the tears that sprang to her eyes. 'You've no call to be sorry for us,' she muttered. 'I tell you, we're managing fine on our own.'

'Yes, I know,' said Jenny gently. 'You're a very brave girl to take such hard knocks and come back fighting. We all admire you tremendously.'

'Don't take no notice of me.' Doris dashed away her tears with the back of her hand. 'It's Mum dying so soon after Dad that makes it so hard to bear.'

Jenny knew that Sam Cottrell had been killed in an accident with a slurry tanker only a few weeks before the baby was born, and her heart was torn with pity for the eldest girl on whose narrow shoulders rested the burden of bringing up the orphaned family.

But Doris wasn't the type to knuckle under easily. 'It's no use moaning and groaning about it,' she declared, and she resumed her digging, leaving Jenny rather at a loss.

'Would you like me to take the children for a walk?' she asked. 'The toddler's being more of a hindrance than a help to you.'

'Let 'em bide,' Doris answered. ''Twould be more of a help if you put in the broad beans.' She handed Jenny a packet of seed and indicated the trenches she had already dug. 'Four inches apart,' she said. 'Just push 'em down with your thumb and cover 'em over with loose soil. Dad always planted his beans in November and he never got no black fly.'

'I'm afraid I don't know much about gardening,' Jenny admitted. 'Does it matter which way up I put them?'

Doris laughed. 'I guess one way's as good as another,' she said. 'You'd best have that old hot water bottle to kneel on or you'll dirty your jeans.'

It was a long and back-aching job and it was nearly half past three before Jenny had put in the last of the beans. By then it was too late to start on anything else and, in any case, a fine drizzle was beginning to fall, so they collected the garden tools and put them away in the shed before going indoors.

'You'll stay for a cup of tea?' Doris asked as she pushed the pram into the kitchen and then helped little Benjamin off with his wellingtons.

Jenny nodded. She didn't want to outstay her welcome but she was anxious to see Linda before she left and she knew the little girl would soon be home from school. She remarked that it was a shame that such a delicate child had to walk nearly a mile in all winds and weathers.

‘ ’Tisn’t so bad now Cliff’s got a motor bike,’ Doris said. ‘He takes her in the morning and fetches her after school.’

‘Oh dear—that doesn’t sound very safe,’ Jenny remarked. ‘I hope she wears a crash helmet.’

‘No need for that. ’Tis an old motor bike and side car Cliff found in one of the farm sheds,’ Doris told her. ‘Dates back to the ark by the looks of it. The Wickhams said he could have it and welcome if he could get it to work. No problem about that. Cliff could get a couple of saucepan lids to take off if he put his mind to it.’

Jenny glanced at her watch. ‘Then Linda won’t be back for some time? Does she wait at the farm till Cliff’s ready?’

‘This time of year he knocks off around four,’ Doris told her. ‘Cynthia says ’tisn’t good for Linda to be out after dark.’ While she was talking she lifted the baby out of his pram and gave him a cuddle. ‘The Wickhams have been real good to us since Dad was killed,’ she continued. ‘ ’Twasn’t nobody’s fault but his own but, ever since the accident, they couldn’t have been kinder. Like when Cliff was in trouble with the police, stealing and vandalizing. Guy gave him a job soon as he left school and he promised Mum he’d keep an eye on him and see he behaved himself. It's not that Cliff's a bad lot—it's just that he got in with the wrong set, and it was difficult with Dad not here to make him toe the line. I sometimes wonder how Benjy and Harry will make out. I'll be able to cope with Linda but what'll I do if I have two more little tearaways on my hands?'

'Don't worry about it till the time comes,' Jenny advised. 'After all, Benjy's only two and Harry's still a baby. You'll be married long before they start giving you any trouble.'

'Some hopes! I can't see any chap in his right senses saddling himself with me and four ready-made kids,' Doris scoffed.

'You could have them taken into care,' Jenny suggested, but, looking around at the spick and span kitchen and the well-fed, well-clothed children, she could see that such an upheaval wasn't strictly necessary. All the same, it would be a shame if Doris's matrimonial hopes were to be dashed because of her responsibilities.

'Over my dead body,' Doris replied, and she clutched the baby more tightly to her bosom. 'Reckon I'm proper daft about Harry,' she admitted. 'And Benjy too. With Mum being ill for such a long time and me having to do everything, I suppose I look on them as my own kids.'

'They certainly do you credit,' Jenny said. 'But I don't think you ought to have to give everything up for them. You're far too young to be tied hand, foot and finger. And I'm sure Linda's a continual source of worry.'

Doris's face clouded over. 'She's all right in the summer but it's the same every winter. She misses so much school she's always at the bottom of the class. 'Tisn't her fault—she's as bright as a button, but I haven't time to help her with her lessons when she's home sick. Doctor Hatherley used to say she'd grow out of her bronchitis when she was seven, but she's going on ten now and she's as bad as ever.'

'It's a pity the cottage is so damp,' Jenny remarked. Even in the warm kitchen there were patches of mould on the walls, and she guessed there would be no heating at all upstairs. 'I would have thought the owner could have done something about it long ago.'

'Dad never liked to ask in case the rent was put up,' Doris told her. 'He did everything himself, like painting and decorating and roof repairs. If I start asking for things to be done I'll probably have to pay through the nose or else be evicted.'

'Do you know who the owner is?' Jenny asked.

Doris shook her head. 'I haven't a clue. I only know the rent collector calls as regular as clockwork every Friday.'

'Why don't you apply for a council house?' Jenny suggested.

'I'm not leaving here,' Doris declared. 'It's

home, isn't it?'

To which statement Jenny could find no answer. In any case she didn't want to upset Doris by entering into an argument, so she tactfully changed the subject and she was playing on the floor with Benjy when Cliff and Linda turned up on the antiquated motor bike.

When the little girl saw Jenny she gave her a frightened look and, running to Doris, she hid her face in her apron. 'Is that the lady from the welfare?' she whispered.

'No, she's not. Whatever put that idea into your head?' Doris answered.

'Sarah Webb says I'm going to be taken away from you and put into a Home,' Linda sobbed. 'You wouldn't let me go, would you?'

Doris pursed her lips angrily. 'No, of course I wouldn't. Sarah Webb is a nasty, stupid little girl and she doesn't know what she's talking about.'

Somewhat comforted by this reassuring reply, Linda detached herself from her sister and smiled shyly at Jenny. 'Have you brought me a present?' she asked.

'Linda Cottrell!' Doris exclaimed in a shocked voice. 'Of all things!' She turned apologetically to Jenny. 'Don't take no notice of her,' she said. 'Everyone's been giving her presents lately—all her aunts and uncles, and the other folk who came to the funeral, and she's getting to expect it.'

'As a matter of fact I have brought you a

present,' Jenny replied. 'One for you and one for Benjy and one for Harry.'

'How about me?' asked Cliff with a grin. He was a good-looking boy, tall and burly for his sixteen years, and Jenny could see he would be a bit of a handful.

'You're a cheeky one, aren't you?' she retorted. 'I daresay your sister will let you have a share of the jam and cakes I've brought and, if you're *very* good, Harry might let you play with his blue rabbit.'

Doris and Linda laughed at his discomfiture and soon they were all sitting down at the kitchen table eating 'doorsteps' of bread and jam, and enjoying the unusual treat of cakes on a weekday.

When it was time for Jenny to go Doris went to the door with her. 'Thanks for coming,' she said. 'I get lonesome sometimes.'

'I'd like to come again,' Jenny answered. 'Is there anything I can do for you in the way of shopping?'

'Most of the tradesmen call,' was the reply. 'Anyway, 'tisn't far to walk to the village.' Doris spoke absently and her mind was obviously on other things. 'What Sarah Webb said about the welfare lady—it's not true, is it?'

'About Linda being taken into care? No, I'm sure there's not a word of truth in it. In any case the authorities would have to discuss it with you first. Don't worry, Doris. From what Doctor Barrett says I gather the whole community will back you up if you want to keep the children. And—Doris, you might like to know I'm a trained nurse and you can count on me to help out if ever any of you are ill. I believe the district nurse is a bit of an old she-dragon.'

Doris nodded agreement. 'We don't see eye to eye over some things,' she admitted. 'She said I wasn't to rub liniment on Linda's chest but Mum didn't hold with medicines. Nor do I. Stands to reason a pill goes straight to the stomach, and I'd like to know what's the good of that when it's Linda's chest and not her stomach that's the trouble.'

Jenny decided it would be pointless to try and explain how antibiotics work, but she was rather alarmed to think that the doctors' prescriptions had probably been consigned to the dustbin. If this was the case it was no wonder Linda's attacks of bronchitis were so prolonged and severe.

'At any rate Linda looks perfectly all right at the moment,' she said, 'but when the weather's bad I'd keep her home from school to be on the safe side. By the way, I don't mind baby-sitting for you sometimes—Saturday would be the best night because there's no evening surgery.'

'Thanks for the offer but nobody's likely to ask me out,' was the rather ungracious response.

'They'll ask you all right if you show willing,' Jenny pointed out, and she reflected that

Doris would look quite pretty if she wore a decent dress and took the trouble to wash her hair. 'Anyway you might bear my offer in mind. There are dances most Saturdays at the village hall and it's about time you had a bit of fun.'

'There's Joe Hawkins,' Doris said. 'I used to go with him 'fore Mum took ill.' Her face fell. 'Daresay he's got another girl by now.'

'I could come on Saturday week,' Jenny coaxed. 'Why not get in touch with him and see what happens? If Joe's not available you're bound to meet up with someone else at the dance.'

'I couldn't go alone,' Doris argued. 'A nice fool I'd look turning up to the dance and being a wallflower all evening. Besides, how'd I get there? 'Twouldn't be much fun cycling two miles in my best dress and probably getting wet through into the bargain.'

'Honestly, Doris!' Jenny exclaimed. 'I'm beginning to think you don't want to go. Surely Cliff could take you on his motor bike and bring you home afterwards?'

'Suppose he could, though I'd rather it was Joe. Thanks a lot then, if you're sure it won't be a trouble.'

The acceptance of Jenny's offer was given rather grudgingly but there was a sparkle of anticipation in Doris's eyes and Jenny had the satisfactory feeling that her visit hadn't been in vain. 'The poor girl,' she thought. 'I don't suppose she's had a single treat for the past six months.'

She had stayed much later at the Cottrells' than she intended and, rather than cycle home in the dark along the country lanes, she cut through to the main road. This took her past the manor and she was surprised to see the house was a blaze of light. 'That's odd,' she thought. 'Alan said the Ashcotts weren't coming back from Canada till the New Year. I wonder why they've changed their plans.'

By now the thin drizzle had turned to a heavy downpour. It was windy too and, despite her anorak, she was soon wet through but she was so late she decided to go straight to the surgery rather than go home first. She hung up her sodden anorak and, hurriedly taking off her jumper and jeans, she put on her overall over her bra and briefs, and she was roughly towelling her hair when, punctual to the minute, the doctor rang his bell for the first patient.

The waiting-room was fuller than usual and everyone seemed to be suffering from coughs and colds. Jenny, who was very inadequately clad, felt as if she was being bombarded by germs every time she put her nose round the door and, by the time the last patient had been dealt with, she was beginning to feel an ominous tickle at the back of her throat. 'I'd better ask Doctor Hatherley to let me have one of his sample medicines,' she decided and she knocked lightly on the door of the consulting-room. To her surprise it was Nigel and not Doctor Hatherley who was seated at the desk, and the taut expression on his face pulled her up short.

'Oh!' she exclaimed, rather inadequately. 'I'm sorry—I thought Doctor Hatherley was on duty.'

He raised an eyebrow. 'If you could only get into the habit of being more punctual you wouldn't have these nasty little surprises,' he said caustically.

'I wasn't late,' she protested.

'Since surgery begins at five-thirty I would hardly call arriving at five twenty-nine being early,' he pointed out.

'I went to see Doris Cottrell,' she defended herself. 'I stayed longer than I meant to and I got wet through cycling home.' His expression didn't alter and she felt angry with him for being so unsympathetic. 'I think I've caught a cold,' she continued. 'I was going to ask Doctor Hatherley to let me have some medicine.'

He jerked his head in the direction of the medicine cabinet. 'Help yourself to the stage properties,' he said. 'There are enough samples in there to treat every illness under the sun but, considering some of them date back to the nineteen twenties, I doubt if they are very effective. Incidentally, if you wore a few more clothes,' he added, obviously aware that she was wearing next to nothing under her overall, 'you wouldn't be so liable to catch a chill.'

'I told you—I got wet through and I didn't have time to go home and change,' she said crossly. 'By the way, what's happened to Doctor Hatherley?'

'If you cast your mind back you may recall that he's attending a medical dinner tonight.'

Her anger ebbed away. Nigel looked tired and overworked and it was no wonder that his temper was frayed at the edges. 'You oughtn't to be such a dogsbody,' she declared. 'Doctor Hatherley takes advantage of you.'

'Well, it won't be for much longer. I've said all along I'll be leaving at Christmas. There's this Houseman's job coming up in January but Hatherley seems to think I'll be willing to turn it down and come in as his partner.'

'I wish you would,' she said impulsively.

He gave her a direct glance. 'Why?' he asked. 'I thought you couldn't wait to see the back of me.'

'That's not true,' she said indignantly. 'I know we rub each other up the wrong way but the patients like you and you seem to fit in here so well. To start with I thought you were stuffy and full of your own importance, but I've since found out I was mistaken.'

'Well now—that's remarkably handsome of you to say so.' Something very like a twinkle appeared momentarily in his eyes. 'Perhaps I will stay on, but it's something I can't decide in a hurry. It depends on a number of things.' He fell silent and Jenny guessed he was thinking about Gwen Ashcott and the complications that would arise if he stayed on as Doctor Hatherley's partner.

'Did you know the Ashcotts are already back from Canada?' she asked, turning round from the medicine cabinet where she had been searching for a box of suitable pills.

By the look in his eye she could see he had followed her train of thought and she could have kicked herself for being so tactless.

'So I understand,' he answered. 'Cynthia phoned me just before surgery to put me in the picture. Apparently Mrs Ashcott has recently had a stroke and she was naturally anxious to come home as soon as she was well enough to travel.' His tone of voice warned Jenny to say no more, but the reason for the strained expression on his face was all too apparent. He had fully intended to leave before the Ashcotts returned from Canada but, now that they had come back to England earlier than expected, a meeting between himself and Gwen was almost inevitable.

What would the outcome be? The disastrous love affair had left him bitter and disillusioned and, judging by his attitude towards the female sex in general, and Jenny in particular, it was clear that time had done little to heal his wounds. He disliked and distrusted all women under thirty, unless they happened to be his patients, in which case professional and humanitarian interests outweighed everything else.

'What a pity Gwen didn't meet somebody in Canada and get married over there,' Jenny thought. 'It would have solved everything. As it is she'll probably try to get her hooks into Nigel again and, if she's as horrid as Cynthia says she is, I can't see much good coming out of that.'

She gave an involuntary shiver, followed by a sneeze, and Nigel looked at her with sudden concern. 'You really have caught a cold,' he said. 'Get along home as quickly as you can and go straight to bed. Those pills won't do you an atom of good.' He took the box from her and dropped it into the waste bin. 'Have a hot lemon drink laced with brandy and, if you take a couple of soluble aspirins, you'll probably be as right as rain in the morning. If not you'd better ask your sister to call in and pick up a prescription for antibiotics. How is she, by the way? I haven't seen her recently so I might as well give her a check up at the same time. I'm hoping she'll be sufficiently recovered to go back to college next term.'

'She jolly well ought to be,' Jenny retorted. 'She's been sitting around like Lady Muck for far too long and, quite frankly, I don't think she wants to go back, though heaven knows what sort of a job she'll get without proper qualifications.'

He gave her an ironic glance and she coloured, knowing that he was thinking about her own failure to complete her training as a nurse. As it turned out she had been fortunate to get a job she liked but Carol might not be so lucky.

'I wish Dad would play the heavy father and made her go back,' she continued, ignoring his unspoken criticism. 'Alternatively *you* might be able to persuade her.'

'I'll broach the subject if I see her tomorrow,' he agreed, 'but I don't want to force the issue. Now that she's leading a more or less normal life it would be too bad if she had a setback. Personally I don't see the necessity for a college education in her case. She's the sort of girl who should stay at home and arrange the flowers.'

'While lesser mortals do the fetching and carrying. Yes, that's Carol all right. One thing's for sure. There'll always be somebody ready and willing to take care of her. If neither of us gets married it's me who'll be the doormat in our old age.' She finished her sentence with another violent sneeze and, having retreated from the surgery and put on her still wet outdoor wear, she reflected dismally that, if she had been Carol, Nigel would have offered to drive her home instead of letting her cycle in the pouring rain.

However, when she got to the door she found him waiting for her in the car. 'I've some calls to make so I might as well give you a lift,' he said, making it very clear that he wasn't putting himself out on her account. 'You can leave your bicycle here until you're fit enough to ride it again.'

'I've got to come in tomorrow,' she declared.

'Nobody's indispensable,' he replied imperturbably. 'Mrs Hatherley can cope with the telephone, and the paper work can be left till you come back.' His tone of voice forbade further argument and, truth to tell, she was thankful to have the decision taken out of her hands. All she wanted to do was to tumble into bed and stay there for ever and ever. 'Remember,' he added, 'if you start taking the antibiotics you're to finish the whole course. No stopping half-way just because you're feeling better.'

This was something he was always at great pains to impress on his patients. 'Yes, Doctor,' she meekly agreed. 'I'll remember. By the way, I think you ought to know that Mrs Cottrell "didn't hold" with pills. From what Doris says it sounds as if her mother used to rub Linda's chest with liniment and throw the antibiotics away.'

For a moment Nigel looked thunderstruck. 'The devil she did!' he exclaimed. 'Thanks for telling me. I daresay Doris doesn't hold with pills either.'

Later that evening Carol came into Jenny's

bedroom with a glass of milk and some antibiotics. 'Nigel brought these for you,' she said. 'He thought you'd better start on them straightaway instead of waiting till morning.'

'That was kind of him,' Jenny croaked, seeing by the label on the bottle that he had had to drive more than five miles to find a chemist shop that was still open. She vaguely wondered why Carol had brought her the pills instead of Morwenna, who usually did all the fetching and carrying, but the reason was soon apparent.

'I've offered to "stand in" for you while you're away from work,' the younger girl said. 'I'm a bit bored hanging around doing nothing and, as I've decided not to go back to college, I suppose I'll have to get a job and earn some money. Daddy's quite generous but I can't keep on asking him, and everything is so expensive.' By 'everything' she meant make-up and clothes: it had certainly never occurred to her that she ought to contribute towards her keep. 'I saw a gorgeous coat the other day but it's a bit pricey and Mummy boggled when I told her and said she couldn't possibly afford to give it to me, especially just now, with Christmas round the corner, and all the extras she's got to buy. So I thought if I took a job I could earn enough to pay for it myself. Meanwhile I shall open a budget account with the store and, if I pay out five pounds, I can spend one hundred and twenty pounds straightaway.'

This was typical of Carol. She could never wait for anything—if she wanted it she had to have it now this very minute. It was a good thing Morwenna had put her foot down for once, because if Carol had to work for her money she might value it more. She had been spoon-fed for far too long and it was high time she started to earn her living. All the same, Jenny wasn't sure that she wanted her sister to take over her own particular job, even on a temporary basis. If Carol found that she enjoyed working as Doctor Hatherley's receptionist she would move heaven and earth to winkle herself in permanently, and she had a way of getting what she wanted. Pressure would be brought to bear on Jenny and, before she knew what was happening, she would find herself back in London again, working at the health clinic. And this was something she certainly didn't want to do. To live at home had become very important. She liked her job very much and, what was more to the point, she had made contact with Alan again.

'I don't think it's a very good idea,' she objected. 'Did Nigel suggest it?'

'No, he didn't. As a matter of fact I had the bright idea myself. It seemed a marvellous opportunity to earn some easy money.' Carol examined her nails which were varnished a rosy pink, the exact shade of her lipstick, and Jenny stifled an envious sigh, remembering how she herself had looked earlier that evening, damp and scruffy and as plain as a pikestaff, whereas Carol always looked as if she had stepped straight out of a bandbox.

'Being a receptionist isn't exactly a piece of cake,' she pointed out, hoping to put her sister off. 'It's jolly hard work.'

'I daresay I'll muddle through all right.' Knowing her own capabilities, Carol gave a self-satisfied smile. 'After all, it's only for a couple of weeks.'

'It had better be,' Jenny thought resentfully as she burrowed her head under the bedclothes. 'If Carol wants my job this is one time when I'll dig my toes in.'

CHAPTER FIVE

Jenny felt worse than ever the next morning and, remembering how ill she had been with glandular fever, Morwenna told Carol to ask one of the doctors to call in and see her sometime during the day. Rather to Jenny's surprise it was Nigel who came and not Doctor Hatherley and, when he had examined her, he diagnosed influenza. 'You probably wouldn't be so ill if you hadn't got wet through yesterday,' he said, looking at her with a worried frown on his face. 'I think I'll have to send you to hospital—Morwenna's not fit enough to nurse you and you do need intensive care. I've been going through your case history and I see you had glandular fever some months ago. I didn't know about this and I feel I owe you an apology. You see, I gathered from your sister that you had opted out of general nursing of your own free will and settled for an easier job.'

He patted her hand and Jenny looked at him in amazement. It was the first time he had ever treated her with such consideration and she wondered what had prompted this sudden change of heart. And then she realized she was now his patient and, being a very sick girl, she could no longer be regarded as a predatory female.

But what on earth had made Carol imply that she had opted out of nursing? If she had deliberately misled Nigel, Jenny would find it difficult to forgive her.

'I'll make the necessary arrangements for getting you into hospital,' he continued, and he wouldn't listen to Morwenna's protestations that she was quite well enough to cope with sick nursing. So, a few hours later, Jenny found herself safely tucked up in a bed in the intensive care unit of the nearest hospital.

For the next twenty-four hours she was too dopey to know much of what was going on but, by Saturday, she was sitting up and taking notice and she was allowed to have family visitors, but only two at a time. First Morwenna and Richard came to see her, both looking worried and anxious, and leaving her in no doubt as to how much they loved her. Then Carol, looking very smart in her new coat, and full of enthusiasm about her job.

'I didn't realize how bored I was staying at home,' she admitted. 'I'm glad I decided to take a job instead of going back to college. All those ghastly exams were a bit of a bind and it would have been at least another year before I graduated.'

'I won't be on the sick list for very long,' Jenny reminded her. 'What sort of a job are you going to apply for?'

'Something local—I couldn't bear to live away from home. But I'm not too worried. Something's bound to turn up. If all else fails I could work in a shop. I'd quite like that. Preferably a florist or a dress shop. Decent hours and quite good pay, though of course I'd rather be a receptionist. It's a pity Doctor Hatherley is the only GP in the neighbourhood.'

'I wish you'd go back to college,' Jenny said persuasively. 'You'd stand a much better chance of getting a really decent job if you had a degree. And think of the money you'd earn.' It annoyed her that Carol was wasting her opportunities. She had inherited a first-class brain from her father and had succeeded in taking two A levels despite missing so much school. Yet she was fully prepared to sacrifice what could be a brilliant career in favour of a run-of-the-mill job which required no qualifications.

'I don't see the point of training for a career when I'll probably get married,' Carol argued. 'Mummy and Daddy bulldozed me into going to college, and I never really wanted to do all that studying. Do stop reading the riot act, Jenny. I didn't come here to be lectured.'

'All right then—please yourself,' Jenny felt too weak to argue. 'By the way,' she continued, 'I've got a bone to pick with you. Why did you tell Nigel I opted out of nursing of my own free will?'

Carol's eyes opened wide. 'I never said anything of the sort,' she fibbed. 'He must have misheard. All I said was that it was a pity you didn't stay on long enough to get your SRN but that was ages ago. Whatever made him bring it up after all this time?'

'Simply because he's only just discovered the truth,' Jenny retorted. 'I think it was jolly mean of you, Carol. No wonder he had such a low opinion of me.'

'Honestly, Jenny! The fuss you make. Anyone would think that Nigel's opinion of you was of world-shattering importance. The trouble is you're too thin-skinned and you blow things up out of all proportion.' Before Jenny could reply to this unjust accusation Carol glanced at her watch. 'I've got to go now,' she said. 'I mustn't keep Mummy and

Daddy waiting any longer. Is it safe to kiss you? I don't want to pick up any of your germs.' To be on the safe side she blew a kiss and departed far more speedily than she need have done. Jenny supposed she should have been honoured by the visit—after all, Carol hadn't been to see Morwenna when she was in hospital—but she guessed her sister had come for the sole purpose of needling her into agreeing to let her have her job.

Tears of weakness trickled down her cheeks and she dashed them impatiently away. 'I won't let Carol get under my skin,' she declared, but the damage was done and she could only toy with her supper. 'What's the use of fighting?' she thought miserably. 'Carol always comes out on top.'

But she cheered up when Nigel called to see her later that evening. 'Oh,' she exclaimed in some confusion. 'What a nice surprise. I didn't expect you to come and see me.'

'I like to keep tabs on my patients,' he said, glancing at the chart at the foot of her bed. 'You appear to be making excellent progress.'

'Yes, I'm much better, thank you. In fact, I feel rather guilty about occupying a hospital bed. How soon can I go home?'

'Don't be in too much of a hurry. If you're worrying about your job—forget it. Carol is managing very nicely and, quite frankly, I'm surprised by her efficiency. She certainly isn't just a pretty face.'

'Carol can excel at anything if she sets her mind to it,' Jenny told him. 'The trouble is she doesn't very often bother.'

He pulled a chair forward and sat down. 'Before I forget I've got a message for you from Doris Cottrell. She's sorry you're ill but she hopes you'll be well enough to baby sit for her next Saturday. She says it's very important.'

Jenny smiled. 'It sounds as if Joe has turned up trumps,' she remarked.

'Joe?'

'Her erstwhile boyfriend. She used to go out with him before her mother was taken ill, but she's been housebound for months and she was afraid he may have grown tired of waiting.'

'So that's why she was looking so cheerful. I expected to find her down in the dumps but she actually greeted me with a smile.'

'I'm glad to hear it. The poor girl has a lot on her mind just now. When I was there the other day Linda mistook me for the "welfare lady" and she thought I was going to take her away and put her in a Home. I could see Doris was worried sick.'

'As a matter of fact I had good news for her and that was why I called to see her. She is going to be allowed to keep the children, at any rate for the time being. She'll be all right financially with National Assistance, and the Health Visitor will call regularly and keep an eye on them. It's a much better arrangement than having the family taken into care.'

Jenny flashed him a grateful look. 'I'm sure you had a lot to do with the authorities making such a humane decision,' she said.

'The chief credit must go to Doctor Hatherley,' Nigel replied. 'I merely backed him up. His impassioned plea on Doris's behalf brought a tear to every eye. Only one opponent refused to give quarter and you can guess who that was.'

'The district nurse?'

He nodded. 'Miss "Brimstone and Treacle" in person . . . If ever a woman was well named . . .'

Jenny giggled. Miss Grimsdyke-Beagle was a newcomer to the district and, although Jenny had never met her, she had heard enough about her to know that the nickname was fully justified, but she had never expected Nigel to unbend sufficiently to share the joke with her. Looking at him sitting beside her in such a relaxed and friendly manner, her heart gave an unexpected jolt and she suddenly realized how fond she had become of him during the past few weeks. 'If only he would stay on,' she thought wistfully and, for a moment, she forgot her involvement with Alan.

'By the way,' he said, as he got up to go, 'I've definitely decided to go into partnership with Doctor Hatherley, so I'll be digging myself in. If you hear of a decent house coming up for sale somewhere in the neighbourhood you might let me know.'

Jenny's eyes shone. 'I'm so glad,' she exclaimed and her obvious sincerity brought a smile to his face.

'Doctor and Mrs Hatherley have made me extremely comfortable,' he continued, 'but living with them was only a temporary arrangement and it's high time I had a place of my own.'

'Don't you think a flat would be easier to run?' Jenny asked. 'Not many bachelors live in a house.'

'I don't see why not,' he replied. 'I'm sure one of the village women would come in and clean for me once or twice a week, and I'm quite capable of doing my own cooking. Besides, I like gardening.'

It didn't sound as if he had any intention of making it up with Gwen and going to live with her at the manor, and Jenny breathed a sigh of relief. She had never met Nigel's ex-fiancée but, for some reason or other, she had taken a violent dislike to the girl and she wished with all her heart that she had remained in Canada instead of returning home to re-open old wounds and disrupt people's lives.

'Why don't you ask my father to let you know if he hears of anything suitable?' she suggested. 'Being a solicitor he's the first to know when a property belonging to one of his clients is coming on the market.'

Nigel nodded. 'That sounds like a good

idea. And I'll ask my cousins to keep their eyes and ears open and let me know if they hear of anything.'

'Are you seeing them tomorrow?' Jenny asked. 'If so, give them my love and tell Cynthia I'll come and exercise Sweet Briar again as soon as I possibly can.'

'You won't be horse riding for at least another week,' Nigel said firmly, 'and even then you must be guided by the weather.'

Jenny turned pale. 'I'm not going to be a permanent invalid, am I?' she asked in sudden fright.

'Good heavens, no. I said a week not a year. You needn't worry about your health, Jenny. In fact, I think the doctor who advised you to give up your nursing career was being over cautious. I presume it was Doctor Hatherley, and you know what an old woman he is. As a matter of fact the severity of your present illness has nothing to do with your attack of glandular fever. It happens to be a particularly nasty strain of influenza and it hit you when you were most vulnerable. To come to the point I see no reason why you can't go back to nursing next year if your heart is still set on it.'

For a moment Jenny closed her eyes and relaxed against her pillows as a wonderful feeling of well being enfolded her. To be told she could qualify as a nurse after all—nothing could have pleased her more. Opening her eyes she flashed Nigel a radiant smile. 'Thank you,' she whispered, almost too overcome for words. 'I'm so happy I feel like bursting into tears.'

He patted her hand in the same way that he patted the hands of old and young alike when they came to him for comfort and reassurance. 'I'll call in and see you again tomorrow,' he said, 'but I don't foresee any complications. All being well you should be able to go home on Tuesday and by Saturday you'll be back to normal.'

'And up will come your defences again,' Jenny thought a little sadly. 'I won't be your patient any longer but a nasty predatory female to be kept at arm's length. Not that I mind,' she comforted herself. 'It's Alan I'm in love with and, for all I care, Nigel can remain a crusty old bachelor for the rest of his life.'

Nigel was right in his diagnosis and there were no further complications, so Jenny was allowed home on Tuesday. A 'get well soon' card from Cynthia was waiting for her and, inside, Alan had scribbled a message:— 'Poor old Jen! Let me know when you're back in circulation and we'll arrange a meeting!' No visit. No flowers. Jenny was disappointed but she wasn't really surprised. Alan wouldn't have any use for invalids and actually she was quite glad he hadn't come to see her while she was in hospital. Her hair had looked a mess and, with no colour in her cheeks, she must have looked terribly unattractive.

Rather surprisingly Carol was still enthusiastic about her job and, when she heard Jenny might be going back to nursing, she begged to be allowed to take over permanently. 'You'll have to wait and see what Doctor Hatherley says when the time comes,' Jenny told her. 'It will probably take several weeks before I'm fixed up, and I'm certainly not going to give up my job straightaway, even to please *you*, so the sooner you get that idea out of your head the better.'

'I do think you're mean,' Carol pouted. 'I need the money.'

'Then take some other temporary job,' Jenny advised her.

'Likc what?' Carol asked.

'Oh, I don't know—charring or something like that. There are always jobs for people who want them.'

Carol tossed her head. 'Thanks very much,' she retorted, her voice sharp with annoyance. '*This* job happens to suit me and, if I have to look around for something else, I shall probably get my nervous complaint back again.'

Jenny was reminded of the little girl who used to hold her breath and go black in the face if she didn't get what she wanted, but they were both grown-up now, and the days of giving in were over. 'Lay off, Carol,' she warned. 'The game's not worth the candle. Even Morwenna's beginning to see through you.'

Carol's face crumpled and she burst into tears. 'Everyone's horrible,' she sobbed and she ran out of the room, leaving Jenny to feel guilty and unhappy, but still quite determined to stick to her guns.

Nigel called in to see her the next day in order to satisfy himself that she was continuing to make good progress, and Morwenna remarked that it seemed strange to have him coming to the house to visit Jenny, instead of Carol or herself. 'We're certainly getting our money's worth out of the health service,' she smiled. 'First it was Carol and then me, and now it's you. Let's hope Richard doesn't take it into his head to follow the pattern.'

'Nigel's signing me off to start work again next Monday,' Jenny told her. 'I'm afraid Carol isn't best pleased about it.'

'She's very naughty to make such a fuss,' Morwenna agreed, 'especially as it won't be for long. Doctor Hatherley says she can take over from you as soon as you leave. I'm so glad you're going back to nursing, Jenny. You were a brave girl to be so philosophical when your chosen career was interrupted.'

Jenny smiled. 'It will be wonderful to get back into my uniform,' she said, 'but it will mean a lot of hard work. I've forgotten half of everything I ever learnt and I'm so rusty about practical matters I expect I'll make an awful hash of the simplest job.'

'Nonsense, Jenny. You're a born nurse and you'll quickly get into the swing of things.' Morwenna hesitated, looking rather embarrassed. 'Meanwhile, don't you think it would be a good idea to have a holiday? It would give you time to revise your paper work and, quite honestly, it does seem a pity to turn Carol out of a job just when she's settling down so nicely.'

'No, Wenna. No. Quite definitely no. I suppose it was Carol who persuaded you to put your oar in? Well, you can tell her you did your best but I remain adamant. And if Dad starts in on me he'll get the same answer.'

Perhaps Jenny was being over-sensitive but she had a feeling that the whole family was ganging up on her. They wanted Carol to be happy and it didn't matter how many people were inconvenienced in the process. Basically this was why Jenny had originally left home and she realized it was a mistake to have come back, however much they made her welcome. 'Thank goodness I can take up nursing again,' she thought, and she was glad she had wasted no time writing to St Cuthbert's, the hospital where she had done the first two years of her training. With any luck she should get an answer to her application within the next few days.

There was no necessity for Nigel to call in again to see her and she was surprised when he turned up on Saturday afternoon. 'I believe you're baby-sitting for Doris Cottrell this evening,' he said. 'How do you propose to get there?'

'It's all organized,' she answered. 'Dad's promised to take me and Joe will bring me home afterwards.'

'Tell your father not to bother and I'll pick you up at about seven. Guy brought Cliff to the surgery this morning with a nasty gash in his leg which needed stitching, and he mentioned Linda was off school with a bad cough, so I'll have to go and see how she is. Doris should have sent for me if she was worried, but I daresay she's pinning her faith in liniment, which won't do her an atom of good. This time I'll see to it that she takes the antibiotics even if it means standing over her and forcing them down her throat.'

'Four times a day?' Jenny giggled. 'Isn't that carrying your professional dedication a bit too far? I'm sorry about Cliff,' she added. 'Is he badly hurt?'

'He needed ten stitches in his leg, and his ankle is so badly bruised he can hardly hobble, but I suppose it might have been worse. Farm accidents are the very devil. You know his father was asphyxiated when his clothes caught in a power-shafter?'

'How horrible!' Jenny looked shocked. 'I never heard the details but Doris said it was his own fault for being careless.'

'Yes, it probably was. There was a court case

and the verdict was accidental death, but there must have been carelessness somewhere along the line or it would never have happened. Alan said he used the slurry tanker the previous day and he swears the power take-off was properly guarded.'

'Are you implying that the accident was Alan's fault?' Jenny asked resentfully.

'No, of course not. Even if Alan had been careless it was up to Cottrell to check that everything was in order before he used the tanker. Nobody was to blame except Cottrell himself, but that doesn't make it any easier for his family to bear, which is why everybody is bending over backwards to help them. Not that Doris is the easiest person in the world to get along with.'

'No, she certainly isn't,' Jenny agreed. 'And one thing's certain—nothing short of a bomb dropped on the cottage is going to make her move.'

'What worries me is that one day the river may burst its banks. The cottage is too close for comfort and it would take the full force of the flood waters.'

Jenny frowned. 'Surely if it was going to happen it would have happened years ago,' she said. 'We get floods in the valley every winter but nobody's ever been drowned.'

'There's always a first time,' he pointed out. 'In any case the situation is different now. When the new paint factory was built last summer a half-mile stretch of the river was diverted and the cottage lies far too close to the new loop for safety. I tell you, Jenny, I won't be happy until the Cottrells have been rehoused.'

Morwenna came into the room in time to hear the tail end of the conversation and, after Nigel had gone, she remarked that he was a GP in a thousand. 'He reminds me of the squires in the old days,' she said. 'He looks after his patients in the same way that a good squire looked after his tenants. It's a pity Mr Ashcott didn't carry on with the old tradition,' she added. 'He owned a lot of property round here but all he cared about was how much rent was coming in.'

Jenny pricked up her ears. 'Do the Ashcotts own the Cottrells' cottage?' she asked. 'If so someone might suggest to them it's high time something was done about it. If it's left in its present state of disrepair it will soon go to rack and ruin.'

'You'd better get Doctor Hatherley to mention it,' Morwenna suggested. 'Carol tells me he has been calling at the manor every day to see Mrs Ashcott, so it would be quite easy for him to bring up the subject.'

'*Every* day? I didn't realize she was as bad as that. Nigel told me they came back from Canada because she'd had a stroke but I understood she was better.'

'The journey overtired her, and her

daughter is very concerned about her state of health.' Morwenna gave Jenny a conspiratorial look. 'Carol says the reason Gwen keeps phoning the surgery is because she is determined to get hold of Nigel sooner or later. Fortunately Doctor Hatherley has always been available but the time will come when Nigel will be obliged to come out of hiding.'

'Do you think Gwen really wants him back again?' Jenny asked.

'It certainly looks like it,' Morwenna replied. 'From all accounts she only went to Canada because she was upset about the broken engagement and I daresay she's hoping he will have simmered down and had second thoughts during her absence. Mind you, this is only hearsay. I've never met Gwen and I don't particularly want to, but Mrs Sawyer is a veritable mine of information and there's nothing she doesn't know about the Ashcotts.'

'She used to work for them, didn't she?' Jenny asked. Mrs Sawyer was a newcomer to the Clayton household, their previous home-help having left to have another baby and, since she had come to work for them, the private lives of their friends and neighbours had become an open book.

Morwenna looked a trifle guilty. 'Richard says I oughtn't to listen to her gossip but I find it absolutely fascinating,' she confessed. 'Tuesdays and Fridays are the highlights of my week and I've come to the conclusion that my own life is remarkably dull in comparison with other people's.'

'I should take what Mrs Sawyer says with a pinch of salt,' Jenny advised. 'I expect she paints a pretty lurid picture of us to the other ladies she "does" for.'

'Oh dear,' Morwenna sighed. 'I hadn't thought of that. I shall have to mind my p's and q's in future or I'll be the talk of the town.'

There was no surgery on a Saturday evening so Nigel was able to call for Jenny punctually at seven o'clock. 'I hope you're well wrapped up,' he said. 'The cottage is a draughty old place.'

'At least the kitchen's warm,' she answered, 'and I don't suppose Doris will expect me to sit in the front parlour. What I'm worried about is having Cliff on my hands all the evening. He can't go to the Youth Club with his bad leg so it looks as if I shall have the doubtful pleasure of entertaining him. It wouldn't be so bad if they had a telly.'

'Not to worry. I've still got some calls to make so I can drop him off at the Youth Club and pick him up again around nine thirty,' Nigel offered and he was rewarded by a grateful smile from Jenny.

When they arrived at the cottage a worried Cliff opened the door and he told them Doris was upstairs with Linda and the little ones. 'You've made a wasted journey,' he said to Jenny. 'Looks like she's not going out after all.

Linda's real bad and Doris says she can't leave her.'

The little bedroom was filled with the sound of Linda's breathing. Nigel took one look at her and, telling Doris to get a steam kettle going, he carried the child downstairs and sat her on his knee in front of the fire. Within a few minutes her breathing quietened and, when she was less distressed, he administered an injection.

'She'll be all right now,' he said reassuringly. 'Fill up a hot-water bottle and put her into a warm bed. Are Harry and Benjy asleep? Then I suggest you hurry up and get ready or Joe won't be best pleased if he's left cooling his heels.'

Doris gave him a reproachful look. 'I can't go out and leave Linda,' she protested.

'Why not?' he demanded. 'Miss Clayton's a nurse and perfectly capable of dealing with any emergency. And you, young man,' he added, turning to Cliff. 'If you think you can hobble as far as my car I'll take you to the Youth Club. Miss Clayton will have enough to do looking after the three children without having you on her hands as well.'

The boy's face lit up. 'Smashing!' he exclaimed. 'Thanks a lot, Doc.'

Nigel caught Jenny's eye and they both hid a smile. Cliff's reading matter consisted chiefly of children's comics and he meant no disrespect, but Doris wasn't going to let him get away with it. 'Manners, Cliff,' she said and, if he had been a year or two younger, she would probably have given him a box on the ears.

Joe arrived shortly after Nigel and Cliff departed and, while Doris got ready, Jenny entertained him to the best of her ability. He was a pleasant young man but so shy she found him hard going, and she was thankful when Doris came downstairs. Dressed up to the nines in a rather tight frock and some cheap jewellery she was a very different Doris from the panic-stricken girl of half an hour ago but, judging by the admiring look in Joe's eyes, she was precisely his cup of tea.

'Have a lovely time,' Jenny said as she waved them good-bye. She peered into the murky darkness, anxious to see what sort of transport Joe was providing, and her worst fears were realized when she saw the outline of a battered truck which he had borrowed for the occasion from his employer—a truck which was generally used to take pigs and cattle to market. Doris wouldn't care—love and excitement would keep her warm and cushion her on her bumpy ride, but for Jenny it would be a jolting experience. 'Never mind,' she told herself. 'It's all in a good cause and surely Doris's happiness is more important than my own comfort.'

She went upstairs to look at the children, who were all peacefully sleeping and then, leaving the kitchen door ajar, she sat by the fire with her knitting. The little matinée jacket she was making for Cynthia's baby was taking shape rather slowly because she wasn't all that keen on knitting, but she was glad she had brought something to occupy herself. She reflected that the evenings must be extremely dull for Doris, with no television or radio, but she supposed you don't miss what you've never had, and no doubt there was always ironing or mending to be done.

'Poor Doris,' she sighed, comparing her life to Carol's who was much the same age. 'Only eighteen and with the responsibility of a whole family on her shoulders. Has Joe any idea of what he'll be letting himself in for if he marries her? She's more like a mother than a sister to the little ones and, if he issues an ultimatum, she'll give him up rather than have them taken into care.'

The fire was warm and presently her head began to nod, and she was falling into a doze when she thought she heard Benjy call out. After she had settled him again she stood by the bedroom window looking out into the garden. The rain had temporarily stopped and a watery moon was illuminating the sodden countryside, etching the trees which stood bare against the skyline, and turning the puddles to silver. Even through the closed window she could hear the noisy waters of the river and she agreed with Nigel that it was far too close to the cottage for comfort. Was it only a fortnight ago she had crossed it by stepping stones? Tonight it was in full spate and she looked with alarm at the angry waters rushing urgently down the hillside. But the banks were high and to her certain knowledge the bridge further downstream had never been swept away.

Going downstairs again she looked around for something to do other than knitting and, opening the cupboard where the children kept their toys, she found an ancient record player and some equally ancient records, dating back to the nineteen-fifties. They had obviously been bought at a jumble sale and she smiled as she looked at the titles. 'Shrimp Boats', 'Lay Down Your Arms', 'Mr Wonderful,' and half a dozen others of the same vintage. 'Almost museum pieces,' she decided, blowing the dust off them.

To start with she couldn't get the record player to work but presently she found a loose connection and, keeping her fingers crossed, she put on 'Mr Wonderful'. Despite some rather disconcerting background noises it came over quite well and she found herself singing in unison, quickly picking up the words and tune. Then came 'Shrimp Boats', 'Lay Down Your Arms', and several of Russ Conway's catchy tunes. But it was 'Mr Wonderful' that she played over and over again, until finally the record player got fed up and grinded to a halt.

Try as she would she couldn't get it going again and at length she gave up and put it back in the toy cupboard.

For want of something better to do she put on the kettle and, when she had made a pot of tea, she took some biscuits out of the tin Doris had put ready for her. Lonely and bored she felt quite hungry and she was wistfully thinking about 'food, glorious food' when Nigel and Cliff returned, bearing with them some fish and chips which they had picked up on their way home from the Chinese take-away.

Jenny added another tea bag to the pot and they all three sat round the fire, eating their fish and chips out of newspaper and laughing and talking with the ease and contentment of old friends. Now and then Jenny saw Cliff looking at Nigel in the same sort of respectful, admiring way that a son sometimes looks at his father, and she thought how tough it was on him that he should have lost his Dad at the very time in his life when he most needed a hand to guide him.

Before he left Nigel went upstairs to look at Linda and, having satisfied himself that all was well with her, he left word that he would call again in the morning. 'Now, young Cliff,' he said, putting on his coat, 'off to bed with you. I'm sorry I've got to go, Jenny, but Doctor Hatherley likes to be in bed by eleven and I don't want him to be disturbed if the phone rings.' He said good-night and Jenny went to the door with him. 'I'm glad the rain has eased off at last,' he remarked, 'but it's going to be a long, wet winter by the look of it.' He said no more, but she knew he was thinking about the river, and her own thoughts echoed his anxiety. The cottage was in a more vulnerable position than any of the other houses in the neighbourhood and it would be the first to be engulfed if the river burst its banks.

'Thank you for taking Cliff off my hands,' she said, 'and the fish and chips just about saved my life. I was absolutely starving.'

He seemed in no hurry to get into the car but stood smiling down at her, and she found his nearness strangely disturbing.

I'll see you on Monday, then,' he said and, after a moment's hesitation, he turned away from her and got into the car. 'It'll be nice to have you back,' he added and, although he kept his tone deliberately light, there was no mistaking the warmth in his eyes. 'Good-night, Jenny.'

He switched on the engine and drove away, leaving her with her feet rooted to the ground. What had come over him, she wondered. She was no longer an invalid, but he was continuing to treat her like a human being instead of a predatory female, and she could have sworn that, for one incredible moment, he had wanted to take her in his arms and kiss her.

CHAPTER SIX

On Monday morning Carol wouldn't come down to breakfast but remained sulking in her bedroom. Morwenna looked unhappy and even Richard was more silent than usual so that, by the time Jenny set off for work, she was feeling guilty and down in the dumps. 'But I won't be bulldozed into giving up my job,' she thought, with an unconscious lift of the chin. 'Carol has had her own way far too long and she's thoroughly spoilt.' Nonetheless, she found herself hoping that her application to return to the nursing profession would meet with a speedy response.

Even if it meant seeing less of Alan it would be worth it—and was Alan so *very* important after all? Her feelings towards him were extremely mixed. Physically she was immensely attracted to him but, somewhere at the back of her mind, lurked an uneasy awareness that the idol of her adolescence had feet of clay. It wasn't only the veiled warnings uttered by Cynthia and Guy and Nigel which caused her to hesitate. She had personal experience of the less pleasant side of his nature. And yet . . . and yet . . . Alan at his most charming was almost irresistible and it was quite possible that one day he would catch her off guard and she would forget her doubts and misgivings and agree to do whatever he wanted.

To prove her efficiency Carol had left everything in the surgery in apple-pie order and Jenny had nothing to do while she waited for the first patient to arrive. On his way to a leisurely breakfast Dr Hatherley poked his head round the door and said how glad he was she had recovered from her illness. 'Don't be in too much of a hurry to go back to nursing,' he advised. 'I still think you aren't strong enough, whatever Doctor Barrett says to the contrary. And that's not sour grapes on my part. I'll be sorry to lose you but that sister of yours shows a remarkable aptitude for this type of work and she'll step easily into your shoes.' From force of habit he asked Jenny to open her mouth so that he could look down her throat and, when he had finished his examination, he hummed and he hawed in his usual abstracted manner.

Jenny reminded herself that this was the doctor who was always over cautious, who handed out certificates like confetti and who cheerfully let himself be led up the garden path by malingerers. He had persuaded her once to give up nursing and she had no intention of letting him persuade her again so, having known him all her life, as a family friend as well as a doctor, she laughed and pulled a face at him. 'You *are* an old fuss-pot,' she said, giving him a hug. 'I'm as strong as a horse. Did you know that Nigel—I mean

Doctor Barrett—hasn't turned up yet and the first patient will be here at any moment. Can you stand in for him if necessary?'

'He left word he had been called out early this morning to deliver Mrs Bond's baby,' Dr Hatherley replied. 'He'll be back shortly and I don't see any reason to give myself indigestion by going without my breakfast. Let the patients wait. It won't hurt them for once.'

It evidently didn't bother him that Nigel would have to go on duty on an empty stomach after having been up half the night. To make matters worse Mrs Bond was a prima gravida and, although she had been told that, at her age, she would possibly have a difficult confinement, she had refused point-blank to go into hospital. But Nigel would cope—he always did—and nothing could be allowed to interfere with Dr Hatherley's nine o'clock breakfast of bacon and eggs.

Shortly after the first patient arrived the phone rang and a girl's voice enquired whether Dr Hatherley would be taking surgery. 'No,' Jenny answered. 'Doctor Barrett takes the morning surgery but Doctor Hatherley will be here this evening. Would you like to make an appointment to see him?'

'I think not,' was the reply. 'I may not be able to manage this evening so I'll leave it for the time being. It isn't an urgent matter.' The caller rang off without giving her name and the next half-hour was so busy Jenny forgot all about the mysterious phone call.

Fortunately Nigel was only ten minutes late and, as he passed Jenny's office, he gave her the thumbs-up sign. 'A bouncing boy and Mrs Bond's fine,' he told her. 'Smuggle me in a cup of tea, will you? And I'll grab something to eat later on.'

Towards the end of surgery Jenny glanced out of the window and she was intrigued to see a new mini drive up and park on the opposite side of the road. The driver—a girl—remained seated but, as soon as Doctor Hatherley drove off in his car, she got out and, crossing the road, she made a bee-line for the glass-fronted surgery door.

Who is she, Jenny wondered with idle curiosity as, instead of going into the waiting-room, the girl came forward to speak to her. Smartly but casually dressed in an expensive sheepskin jacket and perfectly tailored slacks, she was the sort of person who would attract attention wherever she went, not only because her hair was as dark as a gipsy's, her eyes deep blue and long-lashed, but also because she held herself with the poise and assurance of a princess.

Her glance rested on Jenny for a moment, quickly summing up her natural hair style and fresh complexion, and dismissing her as a nonentity not worth bothering about. 'How many patients are still waiting to be seen?' she asked, removing her gloves and glancing at her wrist watch.

Jenny recognized her voice as the one she had heard on the telephone. 'Only one,' she answered, 'but I'm afraid you won't be able to see the doctor this morning.'

The blue eyes flashed angrily. 'And why not, may I ask?'

'Because it's already after surgery hours and, unless it's an emergency, the doctor can only be seen by appointment. Are you a patient of Doctor Barrett?'

'It is quite immaterial which doctor I see,' came the stony reply. 'I originally intended to call this evening and talk to Doctor Hatherley but it so happens I was passing the surgery this morning and it seemed unnecessary to make a special journey later in the day.'

'The doctors prefer to see their own patients if possible,' Jenny pointed out. 'Doctor Hatherley is out on his round at the moment so I suggest you make an appointment to see him this evening.'

'You take rather a lot on yourself, considering you are only the receptionist,' the girl remarked insolently. 'I'm quite sure Doctor Barrett will make an exception in my case and that he'll see me as soon as he has attended to his last patient.'

'Doctor Barrett has been up half the night on a maternity case and he has had no breakfast,' Jenny retorted. 'However, as you're so insistent, if you'll give me your name I'll ask him if he'll stretch a point and spare you a few minutes.'

'My name is Gwen Ashcott,' the girl said, after a moment's hesitation.

Jenny had guessed as much already and, knowing from Carol how reluctant Nigel was to renew their old acquaintance, she found herself in rather a quandary. 'Very well, Miss Ashcott,' she said, 'if you'll go into the waiting-room I'll let you know whether Doctor Barrett will see you.'

Acutely embarrassed, she held herself ready to dash into the consulting-room as soon as the last patient left and, when she had explained the situation to Nigel, he gave an exclamation of annoyance. 'Get rid of her as quickly as possible,' he ordered. 'She is not my patient and she has no right to come here and pester me.'

But Gwen had already come into the room. Ignoring Nigel's angry look she stepped forward with her hand outstretched. 'Nigel,' she purred, 'how nice to see you again after all this time. I'm sorry if I've taken you by surprise but the matter is rather urgent. It's about my mother. You know she has had a stroke?'

'Yes,' he answered with stiff politeness. 'I was sorry to hear about it, but I hardly see it is any concern of mine. She is Doctor Hatherley's patient, and any problems that arise should be discussed with him.'

'Nigel, darling, don't be like that,' she

pouted. 'I wanted to talk to you about getting hold of a full-time nurse for Mother. Relying on the district nurse is proving to be a most unsatisfactory arrangement and, in any case, Mother doesn't like the woman. Doctor Hatherley's a bit of an old has-been and he'd probably come up with the suggestion that we should employ one of his retired matrons who would turn out to be a proper battleaxe. I hoped perhaps you'd know of somebody more suitable. It's not that I don't want to look after Mother myself but life's pretty hectic for me at the moment. You probably know I've been roped in by the Plumpton Players to take a leading part in their next production, and we're rehearsing most evenings.'

They had both forgotten Jenny's existence and she escaped from the room as inconspicuously as possible. 'Honestly,' she thought to herslf, 'of all the unprincipled, shameless girls I've ever come across, Gwen Ashcott certainly takes the prize. I don't know how she had the face to barge into the consulting-room like that, when she was perfectly aware Dr Hatherley wasn't here. She actually waited till he'd driven off on his round to make absolutely certain of button-holing Nigel. Well, I only hope he'll give her a piece of his mind.'

But she had an uncomfortable feeling that, once Nigel got over the shock of seeing his ex-fiancée, he would be like putty in her hands. A girl as beautiful as Gwen had everything going for her and, if she was really set on winning Nigel back, she wouldn't hesitate to pull out all the stops.

Firmly telling herself she was mad to get so steamed up about a situation which was no concern of hers, Jenny marched into the now empty waiting-room and set to work to tidy it up with far more energy than was strictly necessary, and she was quite unaware of the fact that she was getting rid of her aggression by shaking and pummelling each cushion as if it was Gwen Ashcott in person.

The weather over the week-end had been diabolically awful, the drizzle of Saturday turning to torrential rain on Sunday, but today the sun had broken through the clouds and Jenny decided to risk cycling over to the Wickhams' farm to see Cynthia and possibly to ride Sweet Briar who had probably had no exercise for over a fortnight. She also hoped to see Alan who had apparently faded out of her life. Truth to tell she was feeling very browned off with him because, apart from his scribbled message inside Cynthia's get-well card, he had made no attempt to get in touch with her. With Alan it was evidently a case of out of sight, out of mind, and she wondered if he had meanwhile got himself another girl.

Cynthia was looking well and happy and she greeted Jenny with a smile. 'I'm so glad you're better,' she said, 'but I'm not going to let you go riding just yet. Nigel was here yesterday and he told me to put my foot down if you got any stupid ideas into your head, so you'd better give it a miss for another week. Sweet Briar's okay—Cliff's been exercising her for me, so you needn't feel guilty.' She gave Jenny an impulsive hug. 'I'm so excited,' she confessed. 'I think everything's going to be all right. I'm past the half-way mark and, as I lost both the other babies in the third month, my doctor says there's every hope I'll carry this baby full term.'

Jenny returned the hug. 'That's wonderful news,' she exclaimed and, for the next half-hour, they sat by the fire, turning the pages of a catalogue and looking at the pictures of prams and cots and baby baths.

Alan came in while they were still discussing which of the various models would be the most suitable, and Cynthia hastily put the catalogue on one side. 'We won't bore you with baby talk,' she said. 'I don't see you as a father figure.'

'I'm fond of kids,' he remarked unexpectedly. 'In fact I'm quite looking forward to being an uncle.' He turned to Jenny. 'I was going to get in touch with you about coming with us to the point-to-point on Wednesday afternoon. We're all going—Cynthia and Guy and myself and there'd be room for you in the car if you care to come along.'

Jenny's face lit up. 'Thank you, I'd love to come,' she said, immediately forgiving him for failing to keep his promise to make a date with her as soon as she came out of hospital. 'I've never been to a point-to-point. Is Guy riding Baronet?'

'Yes, he is—the lucky devil. Perhaps he'll break a leg or something and ask me to take his place.' He gave a rueful grin. 'Some hopes! But I don't see why not. It's always happening in fiction.'

'If you weren't such a spendthrift you could afford to buy a horse like Baronet for yourself,' Cynthia pointed out with some asperity. 'What time are we leaving? About twelve? Is that all right by you, Jenny? You needn't bother about getting anything to eat because we'll take a picnic lunch.'

The fine weather held and Wednesday turned out to be a perfect day for the races. Even the going was good, despite the recent heavy rains and, although it was almost winter, the air was mild and the sky a cloudless blue.

When they arrived at the race course they went to the stables to inspect Baronet who had travelled by horsebox, and then Guy went off to the changing-rooms, and he reappeared shortly afterwards wearing a brilliant silk shirt in green and yellow quartered colours, and white breeches. They stood around chatting while they waited for the first race to begin and Jenny was staring with open delight at the colourful scene when she caught sight of Gwen Ashcott who was standing with a party of friends a little distance away. Alan saw her at the same time and he immediately waved and went across to her.

'It's that awful Gwen Ashcott with some of the snooty crowd from the Plumpton Players,' Cynthia exclaimed. 'Come on, Guy and Jenny—let's make ourselves scarce.'

But it was too late. Gwen, with her friends in tow, was already coming in their direction and, without being deliberately rude, it was impossible to ignore her.

'Long time no see,' she said in her throaty drawl. 'Cynthia, darling, you're looking positively blooming.' Her glance rested on Cynthia's thickening midriff. 'Where is the sylph of yester-year?' she enquired. 'Do I take it congratulations are in order?'

Cynthia flushed with annoyance. It was hardly the time or place to draw attention to her condition and she had difficulty in making a civil reply. 'Yes, I'm having a baby, if that's what you mean,' she retorted. 'I didn't realize it was as obvious as all that.'

Gwen gave an affected laugh. 'My dear, I have eyes like a lynx. Nothing escapes me. Do you know Bob and Jean? Monica and Dickon? And I mustn't forget Crispin, my gorgeous leading man.' She linked arms with a blond youth and, having performed the introductions, her eyes lighted questioningly on Jenny as if she had just seen her, although it must have been perfectly obvious she was with the Wickhams.

'This is a friend of ours—Jenny Clayton,' Cynthia said.

'Oh yes, of course. Doctor Hatherley's receptionist. I didn't recognize you.' This was hard to believe, considering they had met only a couple of days previously, and Jenny found it difficult to control her irritation. Gwen was an arrogant, insufferable snob, and it was about time she was taken down a peg or two.

Presently Guy made his excuses and went off to the stables to saddle Baronet and, although Cynthia and Jenny would have preferred Gwen's room to her company, it was clear that Alan was determined the two parties should remain together for the rest of the afternoon.

Guy was taking part in only one of the races and this, of course, was the highlight of the day. They all gathered by the rails to cheer him on, and when he came in first, a good length ahead of rest of the field, Jenny found herself clapping as excitedly as Cynthia. Even Alan looked pleased and he admitted he had backed Baronet to win and consequently he would be the richer by more than a hundred pounds. Some of the pleasure died out of Cynthia's face. 'You were a fool to bet when the odds were only four to one,' she declared. 'Think what you'd have lost if Baronet hadn't come up to scratch.'

'He won, didn't he?' Alan gave a triumphant laugh. 'Then I don't know what you're grumbling about. We'll all go out on the town tonight to celebrate.'

'Easy come, easy go,' Cynthia remarked caustically. 'You can count me out.'

'Does the invitation include little me?' Gwen asked. 'I'm at a loose end this evening and I was wondering what to do to amuse myself.'

Alan looked exuberant. 'Terrific!' he exclaimed. 'Where shall we go?'

Jenny saw the blond young man's mouth open and shut like a fish, but although it was obvious he had a previous date with Gwen, he was too well trained to raise any objection. As for Jenny herself, if Alan condescended to ask her to join them—which now seemed most unlikely—she would refine the invitation because she certainly wasn't going to play gooseberry.

By this time Cynthia was positively seething with annoyance. 'Let's get out of here and find Guy,' she whispered and she turned rather too hastily, caught her foot against the railings and sprawled headlong to the ground. She got up, ruefully rubbing her ankle and bewailing the fact that she'd got mud on her coat, but she swore she was all right and she begged everybody not to make a fuss.

However Jenny noticed that her face looked

pale and strained and she was relieved when Guy turned up a few minutes later. 'I think Cynthia ought to go home,' she said in hurried undertones. 'She's had a nasty fall and she's badly shaken up.'

Guy uttered an exclamation of concern and as, by now, Cynthia could no longer hide her distress, he said he would take her straight to hospital for a check up. Jenny would have liked to go with them, but she would have been more of a hindrance than a help and, as the visit to hospital might entail a long wait, she decided it would be more tactful to remain with Alan. The problem of transport was easily solved. Guy would drive Cynthia to hospital in his car and, if Gwen's friends all squashed into Bob's estate car, there would be ample room for Jenny and Alan in Gwen's mini.

'You won't mind going with Bob, will you, Crispin?' Gwen asked, effectively getting rid of her no longer needed escort. 'You have such long legs you'll be much more comfortable in the estate car than the mini.'

Alan's legs were just as long as Crispin's but apparently this didn't occur to her and, to Jenny's annoyance, when the last race was over Gwen led the way to the refreshment tent and they all hung around eating and drinking and wasting a lot of time, while Jenny looked anxiously at her watch and prayed she wouldn't be late for evening surgery.

When they at last set off for home she

wanted to ask Gwen to drop her off first but, as the road led directly past the Wickhams' farm and then the manor, she could hardly insist. Alan invited them to come in while he phoned through to the hospital to enquire about Cynthia and, although Jenny was anxious about her friend's welfare, this meant a further delay. The news wasn't too good. Cynthia would have to remain in hospital overnight and Guy would stay with her for the rest of the evening. However, Alan insisted it was only a precautionary measure and there was no real danger of Cynthia losing the baby.

'It's just as well I decided to go out tonight or I'd have had to put up with a bread and cheese supper,' he said, selfishly putting his own interests first, and he arranged to pick Gwen up at seven-thirty. 'Would you like to come, too?' he asked, belatedly including Jenny in the invitation. 'We could probably make up a foursome with Crispin.'

'No, thank you,' she said, doing her best to speak civilly. 'I already have a date.' 'It's not really a fib,' she added to herself, in an attempt to salve her conscience. 'I do have a date—with myself. I've simply got to wash my hair.'

Rather surprisingly, instead of driving Jenny straight home, Gwen turned in through the manor gates and drew the car up in front of the house. Another car was parked further on, under the trees but darkness had fallen and Gwen didn't notice it. 'Come in a minute,' she said. 'I want to check whether Mother took her medicine at four o'clock. The district nurse was supposed to be calling this afternoon but she probably didn't turn up. The woman's a complete fool and I can't rely on her for anything.'

'I oughtn't to stop,' Jenny objected. 'I'm afraid I shall be late for surgery as it is.'

'What a fuss—as if five minutes could make any difference!' Gwen brushed her objection aside and led the way into the house while Jenny followed rather hesitantly. The hall was in darkness but, when Gwen switched on the light, the beautiful cut-glass chandelier sprang into prominence, sending a cascade of brilliance to illuminate every corner of the room, as well as the magnificent staircase which Jenny remembered from her clandestine visit with Alan a few weeks ago.

'Mother will be in the library—it's the warmest room in the house,' Gwen said and she pushed open the door and went into a small but beautifully proportioned room, where a log fire was burning brightly.

Two chairs were occupied. In one sat a slender woman in her early fifties, whose prematurely white hair was arranged in a soft wave across her forehead. Her fine boned face bore traces of her recent illness, but her eyes were serene and her hands lay quiescent in her lap. Beside her chair rested an ebony stick with an ivory handle and Jenny guessed that

Gwen's mother would not be able to venture far without its support.

The occupant of the other chair put down the cup of tea he had been drinking and rose to his feet as Gwen and Jenny came into the room. It was Nigel Barrett. He gave Jenny a friendly nod but his tone was icy as he greeted the other girl.

'Miss Grimsdyke-Beagle phoned through to the surgery and asked me to call,' he said. 'She was worried about leaving your mother alone in the house and she had no idea where she could get hold of you.'

'That woman's a born troublemaker,' Gwen declared angrily. 'Mrs Paget said she'd stay till three o'clock and I thought I'd be home soon after four. Surely Mother can be left for an hour on her own without everybody running round in circles.'

'It happens to be nearly five-thirty,' he pointed out.

'I know I'm later than I meant to be, but it couldn't be helped.' The lie slipped easily off Gwen's tongue but she had the grace to avoid Jenny's reproachful look. 'Perhaps you can see now how important it is to get hold of a nurse to live in as soon as possible. I'm busy with rehearsals most evenings and I can't be expected to be tied hand, foot and finger to a helpless invalid.'

It was a cruel thing for the girl to say in front of her own mother and Jenny's glance flew to the pathetic figure seated in the fireside chair. For a once active woman to be brought to such a pass as this was a tragedy indeed and all Jenny's nursing instincts rose to the surface. Mrs Ashcott needed tender, loving care and attention. Instead she had to put up with nothing but harsh words from a resentful daughter.

'Yes, I do see that a resident nurse is essential,' Nigel agreed. 'As a matter of interest, what arrangements do you make at the moment when you go out in the evening?'

'Mrs Paget lives in and she is always here except on Wednesdays and Saturdays,' Gwen replied. 'Really, Nigel what is this catechism in aid of?'

He ignored the question. 'I presume you have somebody to take Mrs Paget's place when she isn't here?' he asked.

'Yes, of course I have.' Gwen made no attempt to conceal her rising anger. 'Mrs Pike comes in whenever I need her and she holds the fort till Mrs Paget gets back. I assure you, Nigel, Mother isn't neglected, but I'd be much happier if a full-time nurse was in charge. I contacted several agencies, as you suggested, but they seem to think there isn't a hope of getting anybody till after Christmas.'

'They're probably right,' Nigel agreed. 'Meanwhile you'll have to manage as best you can, but please remember you are on no account to leave your mother alone in the house.' He turned to Mrs Ashcott who had apparently not been listening to the conversation, and he patted her gently on the shoulder. 'I'll say good-bye, Mrs Ashcott. And by the way.' He drew Jenny forward. 'I'd like you to meet Jenny Clayton.' The serene eyes smiled at Jenny who knelt impulsively and took the older woman's hands between her own. 'She can hear what you say,' Nigel continued, 'but her power of speech has gone.'

'Would you like me to come and see you sometimes?' Jenny asked. 'I could read to you and we could play card games and do jigsaw puzzles.' Mrs Ashcott nodded and her lips moved, though no sound came. After a moment Jenny got to her feet. 'I shall look forward to coming,' she said and Gwen gave a hard little laugh.

'Quite the good samaritan, aren't you?' she remarked. 'I'll let you know if I need you and perhaps we could come to some financial arrangement. I believe you could be quite useful to me.'

Jenny flushed. 'I would come as a friend, not as a paid companion,' she said stiffly, 'and I'm afraid it couldn't be on a regular basis. I work unsocial hours and I have several other commitments.'

'Oh, well.' Gwen shrugged. 'It was just a passing thought. But by all means come when you can. Mother seems to have taken a fancy to you. By the way, Nigel, you might drive

Jenny home. I'm in a bit of a rush and it will save me an unnecessary journey.'

'I didn't know you were acquainted with Gwen,' Nigel remarked as Jenny got into the car.

'I'm not, really,' she answered. 'I met her for the first time at the surgery on Monday but I was at the races this afternoon with the Wickhams, and Gwen and her party joined us. Unfortunately I had to rely on Gwen to bring me home because Cynthia had a bad fall and Guy took her to hospital. I'm really worried about her. I do hope she'll be all right.'

A look of concern crossed Nigel's face. 'That's bad,' he exclaimed. 'I'll drop you off at the surgery and then I'll drive over to the hospital to find out how she is. You're running it a bit fine, aren't you?' he added. 'It's lucky it's Doctor Hatherley and not me who's on duty or you'd be in dire trouble.'

'It's Gwen's fault I'm late,' Jenny told him. 'She's the most infuriating girl I've ever met. Quite frankly I can't think why you ever got engaged to her.' She spoke impulsively, then, remembering that fools rush in where angels fear to tread, she broke off, biting her lip.

'I fell in love with Gwen for the usual reasons, I suppose,' he answered. 'She's incredibly attractive and, in those days, I was blind to her faults.' He fell silent and, seeing the uncompromising set of his jaw, Jenny was afraid to pursue the subject. The fact that he was no longer blind to Gwen's faults did not necessarily mean he no longer found her attractive, and any further criticism on Jenny's part might be met with a cool response.

The silence between them lengthened but, as they neared the end of their journey, Nigel came out of his reverie and remembered Jenny's existence. 'As a matter of interest,' he said, 'how did Alan get home from the races? Somehow I can't see him travelling in the horse box with Baronet.'

'Gwen gave us both a lift and she dropped Alan off at the farm,' Jenny replied. 'He's picking her up later this evening and they're going out for a meal to celebrate his winnings.' Try as she would she couldn't control the telltale wobble in her voice. Everyone had warned her Alan was a flirt but this was the first time he had given her the brush-off and she found the situation difficult to bear. 'He backed Baronet to win and he raked in over a hundred pounds.'

Nigel whistled. 'He must have bet pretty heavily to have pocketed that sort of money,' he commented. By now they had arrived at the surgery and Jenny opened the car door, hoping he hadn't noticed how upset she was, but she had underestimated him. 'Look, Jenny,' he said. 'Don't waste your tears on Alan. He isn't worth it. We've all warned you, often enough. With Alan everything's a nine-days' wonder and, once he's got what he wants, he couldn't care less. Pay him back in his own coin and don't ever let him guess you're nursing a broken heart.'

She blinked back her tears. 'I've got me "proide",' she said in broadest cockney. 'Actually he asked me to go with them tonight but I said I'd already got a date.'

'Good for you,' he applauded. 'Incidentally —*have* you got a date?'

She shook her head. 'Not really. I'm going to wash my hair and go to bed early.'

His glance rested on her shining copper-nob. 'It doesn't look as if it needs washing,' he remarked. 'How about coming out with me instead? I think we could both do with a boost to our morale. How about it, Jenny? I'll call in at the hospital to enquire about Cynthia and then I've a few other calls to make, but I could pick you up about eight o'clock and we could have a meal out somewhere.'

Jenny hesitated. Did he really want to go with her, she wondered, or was he just being kind? Alternatively, it could be his way of thumbing his nose at Gwen. 'We're two of a kind,' she thought and, quite unexpectedly, she experienced a sudden uplifting of the spirit.

'Terrific,' she said, and her lovely smile shone out like a beacon. 'Golly—look at the time! I must dash or even Doctor Hatherley will be reading the riot act.'

She ran up the path and when she reached the surgery door she turned to wave to Nigel before he drove off. 'You can go and get stuffed, Alan Wickham,' she declared, flinging off her coat and putting on her overall. 'You can marry the lady of the manor, the Queen of Sheba or Lady Godiva if you like. I'm not the slightest bit interested in your love life.' And, firmly putting him out of her mind, she threw open the waiting-room door and called out the name of the first patient.

CHAPTER SEVEN

Immediately after surgery Jenny rushed home to get ready for Nigel and she decided to put on all her fine feathers for the occasion: a sleeveless turquoise dress which she had bought with Alan in mind, elegant high-heeled sandals; an up-to-the-minute shawl of *diamanté* lace. Finally, as a finishing touch, she piled her shining hair on top of her head and fastened it with a *diamanté* comb.

When Nigel saw what trouble she had taken with her appearance he hastily altered his original plans and, instead of dining and wining her at a quiet restaurant, he decided to take her to the most expensive hotel he could think of. Jenny's eyes stood out on stalks when he escorted her into the foyer and she hung back, declaring she didn't want him to spend such a lot of money on her, but he merely laughed and said he had been waiting a long time for such an occasion.

The waiter showed them to a small table in a dimly-lit alcove and hovered discreetly while they studied the king-sized menu. To an outsider it might have looked as if the stage was set for romance, but Nigel made it clear from the outset that he had no intention of standing in for Alan. And Jenny was in much the same position. She had no wish to act as Gwen's understudy and, although she had paid Nigel the compliment of making herself look as attractive as possible, she had no ulterior motive in doing so. She and Nigel were friends—that was all—and, as friends, they could enjoy each other's company, with no strings attached.

Nigel proved to be an entertaining conversationalist. Having set her mind at rest about Cynthia, whose threatened miscarriage had been safely averted, they discussed books, poetry, art and the theatre—even politics—and a wide range of other subjects. Towards the end of the meal, mellowed by good food and excellent wine, the talk inevitably became more personal and he told her he was house hunting in earnest but hadn't yet come across a suitable property. 'They're either too small or too big or else in a shocking state of disrepair. Even the Cottrells' cottage compares favourably with some of the places I've looked at.'

'How depressing,' Jenny sympathized. 'But don't be discouraged. Something's bound to turn up sooner or later. By the way, how is Linda?'

'Well on the road to recovery, I'm glad to say. Mind you, it was lucky you told me about Doris's aversion to pills. I put the fear of God into her, since when she's been dosing the child with clockwork regularity.'

Jenny smiled. 'I must get in touch with her again and offer to baby-sit, but next time I'll get Dad to pick me up and bring me home.' She told him about the cattle truck and he laughed at her description of the bumpy ride. 'A camel would have been more comfortable,' she declared. 'I was positively black and blue by the end of the journey, but it didn't seem to have any ill effect on Doris. After dancing for four hours and being bounced in the cattle truck there and back again, she still looked as fresh as a daisy. Ah me! What love will do for a girl.'

'Perhaps Joe will take the plunge and ask her to marry him,' Nigel suggested. 'It would be one way of getting Doris out of the cottage.'

Jenny shook her head. 'Joe's living in lodgings at the moment, so he'll probably move in with them without bothering to get married,' she said. 'It would be a good arrangement because Doris needs a man about the house and Cliff's too young to be much use to her.'

'Yes, that's all very well,' Nigel replied, 'but think of the gossip. It would be sad if Doris lost the goodwill of the community, though, with all the wife-swapping and other activities that go on in the village, I wonder who would dare to cast the first stone. Nonetheless, a word of warning in Doris's ear wouldn't come amiss. Unless she adheres strictly to the ten commandments the children could be taken away from her and put into care.'

'That's absolutely disgraceful,' Jenny protested. 'Why does the underdog always get treated so badly? Doris is even afraid to ask to have anything done to the cottage in case she gets evicted. Incidentally, did you know the Ascotts own the cottage? It's a pity they don't do something about keeping it in good repair.'

'No, I didn't know, but I'll ask Gwen to speak to her estate manager about it, though I doubt if anything will be done. I daresay the Cottrells only pay a peppercorn rent and this would hardly cover the cost of labour and material.'

'So what? The Ashcotts have pots of money. Morwenna says Mr Ashcott was a tight-fisted old curmudgeon, but I wouldn't have thought Mrs Ashcott was like that.'

'Indeed she isn't.' Nigel spoke with genuine warmth. 'I've always had a great admiration for Mrs Ashcott. The lady has style. Yes, even now, she has style. But you saw for yourself what nature has done to her. She can no longer have any say in the running of the estate.'

'Then it's up to Gwen to see that her manager does his job properly,' Jenny retorted. 'Yes, I know she's only been home from Canada for a short time, but that's no excuse.'

Nigel's lips twitched with amusement. 'I fancy you've missed your vocation,' he chuckled. 'You should have been a schoolmistress.'

Feeling rather deflated Jenny lowered her voice. 'Sorry,' she said. 'I know I shouldn't get so het up but that girl Gwen just about gets my goat.'

'I thought the whole purpose of our evening together was to forget Gwen and Alan,' he reminded her.

'Yes, so it was . . .' Her voice trailed away uncertainly as her gaze by-passed him and alighted on the couple who were seated at a table a little distance away. 'But it's going to be rather difficult considering they've decided to camp out on the same territory.'

He followed her glance and his mouth tightened with annoyance. 'Chin up, Jenny. Don't let him see you care,' he counselled, and he covered her hand with his. 'Shall we dance?'

The orchestra was playing a well-known melody and the couples on the dance floor were drifting round on a bright cloud of music.

Jenny blinked back her tears and flashed him a grateful smile. A moment later she was in his arms and, without conscious effort, their steps matched as if they had been dancing together all their lives. It was a wonderful boost to her morale and, when they returned to their table, she attracted Alan's attention by waving to him in a carefree manner.

His brow darkened when he saw who she was with, because he had already earmarked Jenny for himself and it had never entered his head that he might have competition from his cousin. He had always known that sooner or later he would have to get married and settle down, and now it seemed likely that it would be sooner rather than later, because Gwen apparently quite liked the idea of having him as her new estate manager. When Buckleigh retired the house would fall vacant and Alan would automatically move into it, so the job was more suitable for a married man than a bachelor, and Jenny would make an admirable wife. Therefore Nigel must be told in no uncertain terms to keep off the grass.

Turning to Gwen he asked her if she would like to join the others and she eagerly agreed because she, too, was equally put out at seeing Nigel with Jenny.

'What are you two celebrating?' she asked, smiling with honeyed sweetness at Jenny. 'I couldn't believe my eyes when I saw it was you.'

'Why not?' Nigel asked, rising to his feet. 'You can't expect us to spend all our lives ministering to the sick.'

'Well, I must say it's nice of you to give Jenny an occasional treat,' Gwen remarked in her superior fashion. 'How about changing partners for the next dance?' She held out her arms as the orchestra struck up the opening bars of an old-fashioned waltz, and Nigel could hardly refuse the invitation without being openly rude. This meant that Jenny was obliged to dance with Alan, who she sensed wasn't in the best of tempers.

'I had no idea you and Nigel were such friends,' he remarked in a belligerent tone of voice. 'How long have you been going out with him?'

She wasn't going to tell him this was the first time, so she laughed and made an evasive answer.

'I thought you were supposed to be *my* girl,' he continued. 'I had the distinct impression we had something going for us the other night.'

'The "other" night was more than a fortnight ago,' she pointed out. 'A lot of water has flowed under the bridges since then.'

'It's not *my* fault you were ill,' he said defensively. 'I suppose you're jealous because I invited Gwen to come out with me this evening. You needn't be. I've only been cultivating her because I want Buckleigh's job. Quite honestly, darling, she doesn't mean a thing to me. Which is just as well,' he added, glaring in Nigel's direction. 'The way Gwen's behaving the sun rises and sets with my cousin.'

Jenny wanted desperately to believe him. After all it could be a perfectly genuine excuse because, if he had been spending his time chasing after Gwen with a view to getting the job of estate manager, it would account for his seeming neglect. But it was a moot point and she was still mulling over whether or not to forgive him when she felt his hand move caressingly across the small of her back. Against her better judgement she was beginning to respond when, across the crowded room, she saw Nigel watching her with a sardonic look on his face. 'Stop it, Alan,' she said in a fierce whisper. 'You're not going to get round me as easily as all that.'

'I meant what I said about getting married,' he whispered. 'Remember—we plighted our troth under the kissing tree, and I intend to hold you to your promise.'

The close physical contact, the warmth of his breath fanning her cheek, the ardour with which he spoke, made her feel almost faint. 'I don't know, Alan. Honestly I don't know,' she faltered. 'Marriage is such a big step to take and I don't think I'm ready for it.'

He misinterpreted her meaning and looked at her with the bold tenderness she found so disquieting. 'You were ready the other night,' he reminded her. 'More than ready, I would say.'

Mercifully at that moment the music stopped and, with heightened colour, Jenny led the way back to the table where the others joined them almost immediately. Gwen insisted they should make up a foursome for the rest of the evening and Alan, still flushed with his winnings, ordered champagne all round, but Jenny noticed that, although Nigel had partaken very sparingly of the table wine, he took only a token sip of champagne and he eyed Alan's brimming glass with marked disapproval.

The cabaret came as a welcome diversion and Jenny was able to sit back and relax as a group of African dancers gave a riveting performance. Everybody applauded enthusiastically and the steel drums were beginning to beat out their exciting rhythm in readiness for an encore when there was a sudden disturbance in the foyer and a frantic voice called for a doctor. Apparently two cars had collided head-on just outside the hotel. One car had burst into flames and the other had ploughed into a bus queue, crushing one man against a wall. The driver of this car was badly injured, and his front seat passenger had been thrown through the windscreen and was bleeding profusely.

Nigel immediately got to his feet and, to save precious time, he handed his keys to Alan and asked him to fetch his medical bag from his car. Then he hurried out of the hotel, with Jenny following close at his heels.

A scene of chaos and confusion greeted them as they picked their way across broken glass to examine the injured. The girl, who was lying bleeding on the pavement, needed their urgent attention and Nigel brusquely asked an onlooker to hand over his scarf so that he could apply a tourniquet. Then Alan arrived with Nigel's medical bag and, while Jenny took the crushed man's blood pressure, Nigel gave him a brief examination.

'He's got quite a few broken ribs,' he said, gently probing the thorax. 'How's his blood pressure? Yes, I thought so. His peripheral circulation is terrible. He'll have to have surgery straightaway. Has anyone sent for an ambulance?'

'On its way, Doctor. Can I do anything to help?' A young medical student pushed his way through the crowd and Nigel gave him a nod of recognition.

'Glad to see you, Cooper,' he said. 'Take a look at the girl and loosen the tourniquet while I see to the driver. He looks to be in a pretty bad way.'

Jenny had already crawled into the car and undone the injured man's jacket and shirt, disclosing a widespread bruise by the left lower ribs. 'His blood pressure's right down,' she said. 'Ninety over nothing. I think he's got a ruptured spleen.'

'You're quite right. His peritoneal cavity's awash with blood. Frankly I don't rate his chances of survival very high but an immediate transfusion may save him.' He shone his pencil torch into the man's eyes. 'A pity he wasn't breathalysed,' he commented. 'One thing's certain—there'll be one less menace on the roads, perhaps not permanently, but for a very long time. God! What a massacre! And all so unnecessary.'

The four occupants of the burnt-out car had been dragged clear of the wreckage but they were beyond human aid, and Nigel devoted his whole attention to supervising the lifting of the injured onto stretchers. Turning to Jenny, who would have faded quietly out of the picture, he asked her to stay and comfort the badly shocked girl on her journey to hospital. 'Calm her down while I give her an injection,' he said. 'Did Cooper loosen the tourniquet? Yes, that's fine. Find her pulse while I check up on the crush case. I hope he'll make it, poor devil, but it's touch and go.'

Arriving at the hospital the ambulance unloaded the patients into the casualty department. Fortunately it was an off-peak period and the young houseman and two duty nurses were free to deal with the three emergencies. Nigel could have left with a clear conscience but he decided to stay, at any rate until the crush case had been taken to theatre, and Jenny said she would wait for him in reception and they would share a taxi to take them back to the hotel. However, there was no need for this. The young medical student had followed them in his car and he waylaid Jenny and offered her a lift.

'Thank you,' she said gratefully. 'I don't expect Doctor Barrett will be more than a few minutes.'

Cooper fetched two cups of coffee and came to sit beside her. 'It was jolly decent of you to help,' he remarked, 'especially as you were out of uniform.' Obviously he had taken it for granted that she was a fully qualified nurse and, for the first time, she became aware of her bedraggled appearance. There was blood on the bodice of her dress and the skirt was torn and mud-stained where she had knelt in the dirt beside the injured girl. 'I look a proper mess,' she exclaimed, half laughing. 'I can't think what the head waiter will say when he sees me.'

'It's a rotten shame,' the young man sympathized. 'Your evening's been completely spoilt.'

'It doesn't matter,' she assured him. 'I'm glad I was around to help.'

'You nurses,' he said. 'I take my hat off to you. You do all the dirty work and we doctors get all the praise.'

She was amused by the way he said 'we doctors'. He couldn't have been much more than twenty and he had a long way to go before he qualified, but he obviously already considered himself a fully fledged member of the medical fraternity.

'Thank you, Doctor Cooper, for those kind words,' she said. 'When I'm coping with bedpans and blanket baths and intravenous drips, it will be nice to know that I'm appreciated in some quarters. Most doctors look down their noses at nurses, or else ignore them completely.'

'I'll never do that,' he said earnestly. 'Not even when I'm a consultant.'

Nigel appeared a few minutes later and gratefully accepted the offer of a lift. 'Nice of you to hang around,' he said. 'I hope you learnt something from this evening's drama. Casualties on the pavement are always more traumatic than in hospital.'

'It's the first time I've seen a crush case,' Cooper admitted. 'I thought you were going to diagnose hypovolaemia.'

Nigel didn't blame the young man for airing his knowledge and he tactfully hid his amusement. 'It's difficult to make a true diagnosis without an X-ray,' he said, 'but I was pretty certain it wasn't hypovolaemia. In crush cases you often get bilateral rib fractures which lead to respiratory insufficiency, and then you get mediastinal flap and peripheral hypoxia.'

Cooper nodded. 'Oh, well—you live and learn,' he said cheerfully. 'What are the chances of the patient recovering?'

'About fifty-fifty, I should say. Fortunately he's comparatively young. The girl will be all right but, as for the drunken driver, I would say his chances are practically nil. Poetic justice. He killed those four young men in the burnt-out car as surely as if he'd held a gun at their heads.'

When they got back to the hotel Nigel told Jenny to fetch her coat and he would drive her home. 'I'm sorry the evening had to end like this,' he said, 'but I'm sure you don't feel like dancing any more than I do. Besides, we hardly look presentable enough for public scrutiny.'

Jenny gave a rueful smile. 'Fancy dress would be all right,' she said. 'I could go as a scarecrow.'

He made no comment but his glance assessed the damage done to her fine feathers. 'Alan and Gwen are probably wondering what's become of us, so I'd better put them in the picture,' he remarked. 'When you're ready, wait for me in the foyer—I won't be long.'

He came back almost as soon as she had fetched her coat. 'You forgot your shawl,' he said, handing it to her, 'so at least one of your possessions has escaped damage, but I'm afraid your dress is a complete write-off.'

'Oh well! Next time I come out with you I'll make a point of wearing my uniform—just to be on the safe side,' she said.

'Then your application has been accepted?

Congratulations. I must say that, after tonight's performance, it's abundantly clear that the sooner you get back to nursing the better. You're completely wasted in your present job—in fact, I don't think I have ever worked with a nurse who showed more initiative . . .' he paused 'and compassion.'

Praise from Nigel was praise indeed. Her ruined dress, her spoilt evening—these counted as nothing in view of the way he was looking at her. 'I'm starting at Saint Cuthbert's in February,' she told him. 'If I sweat my guts out it won't be long before I'm Jenny Clayton. SRN. And just think! If it hadn't been for your good advice I would probably have stayed put as Doctor Hatherley's receptionist for the rest of my life.'

Nigel paused fractionally before replying. 'I very much doubt it,' he said, and he slung his bag into the back of the car and got in beside her, but he said no more and she spent much of the journey home wondering what he meant by his enigmatic remark.

The house was in darkness and she pulled her purse out of her coat pocket and fumbled for her front door key. He leaned across and took it from her. 'I'll see you safely inside,' he said and, getting out of the car, he came round and opened the door for her. She stepped out but, during the course of the hectic evening, the heel of one of her sandals had become loose and she stumbled and pitched forward into his arms. He steadied her and set her firmly on her feet, making no attempt to take advantage of the situation but, for one breathtaking moment, the atmosphere between them was charged with emotion.

'I'm sorry,' she stammered, afraid that he would think she had been leading him on. 'My wretched heel—I think it's come off.'

'I didn't imagine you had thrown yourself into my arms on purpose,' he responded, with a hint of irony in his voice. 'You'd better take both your shoes off. I can't have you leaning on me as you hobble up the path, or the local gossips will think I've brought you home in a drunken condition.'

Jenny giggled to hide her embarrassment. 'I do look rather the worse for wear,' she remarked.

'And that, if I may be allowed to say so, is the understatement of the year,' he said in an amused voice. He opened the front door and handed the key back to her. 'Good-night, *Nurse* Clayton,' he said. 'Sleep well.' And, without prolonging the leavetaking, he turned on his heel and strode off down the path.

Feeling curiously light-headed, Jenny tiptoed upstairs, hoping the rest of the household was asleep, but Carol's light was still on and she came bursting out of her room, her eyes alight with curiosity. 'Whatever's happened?' she demanded. 'Has there been an accident? You look terrible.'

'Hush, you'll wake the others,' Jenny whispered and she pulled Carol into her bedroom and hurriedly explained about the car crash and how she had been roped in to help. Carol insisted on being told everything, down to the last gory detail and, even after Jenny was undressed, she still lingered.

'Did I see Nigel giving you a fond embrace when you got out of the car?' she asked.

'No, you didn't,' Jenny retorted. 'My heel had come loose and I tripped and nearly fell. I don't know what's come over you lately, Carol. Listening to telephone conversations and peeping out of windows. It's like having a private eye on my tail.'

'I'm only *interested*,' Carol replied. 'Mummy and Daddy were thrilled to bits when Nigel asked you to go out with him this evening. You may not know it but they've been worried sick about you having such a crush on Alan. They'd much rather have Nigel for a son-in-law.'

'I do wish people wouldn't discuss my affairs behind my back,' Jenny said, rather crossly. 'I'm not thinking of marrying anybody at the present time. All I'm interested in is going back to Saint Cuthbert's and getting my SRN.'

Carol had been jolted out of her usual selfish complacency by the sight of Jenny's blood-stained and bedraggled appearance and she now gave her sister a sudden, unexpected hug. 'I know I'm a beast to you sometimes, but

I do love you,' she said. 'Please marry Nigel. He'll make a super brother-in-law. I used to think I rather fancied him myself but he's much too old for me, so you can have him and welcome.'

'We're just friends,' Jenny replied, a shade too quickly. 'Dad and Wenna are very foolish if they're trying to read anything more into it. Do go to bed, Carol. I'm all in.' And, with a decisive gesture, she switched off the light and lay down.

Jenny wasn't altogether surprised when Gwen phoned her the next day to remind her about her promise to come and sit with Mrs Ashcott. Suspecting it was more for Gwen's own convenience than her mother's, she wasn't very forthcoming. 'When do you want me?' she asked.

'I was hoping you might be free on Saturday,' Gwen replied. 'It's Mrs Paget's day off and unfortunately Mrs Pike has fixed up with her husband to go and see some relatives. It's too bad of her because she knows perfectly well I like to go out on Saturdays.'

'I'm sorry,' Jenny said firmly, 'but it's quite out of the question. I've promised to baby-sit for Doris Cottrell.'

'How frightfully annoying.' Gwen sounded very put out. 'Couldn't you tell Doris you've got another engagement?'

Jenny felt her hackles rise. 'No, I couldn't,' she answered. 'You'll have to get hold of someone else. Or perhaps,' she added scathingly, 'you could stay at home for once in your life.'

Gwen ignored this suggestion. 'What time are you going to Doris's?' she asked.

'Round about seven o'clock, but I don't see what that's got to do with it,' Jenny retorted. 'I've already told you I can't come on Saturday.'

'Oh, but I'm sure we can think of a way out of the difficulty if we put our minds to it,' Gwen said persuasively. 'Actually I'd arranged to go to the theatre with Crispin in the evening but he may be able to get seats for the four o'clock matinée instead. It's a nuisance, of course, but it can't be helped. I suggest you get here by three o'clock and stay with Mother until we get back at about seven. Then I'll ask Crispin to drive you over to Doris's and he can come back here for supper and we can spend the evening rehearsing. This means that Mother won't be left alone for a single moment, and I don't see how even Nigel can find fault with such an arrangement.'

Jenny was left speechless by the cool assumption that she would be willing to fall in with Gwen's plans and, taking her silence for consent, Gwen said she would expect her not a moment later than three o'clock on Saturday, and she rang off before Jenny could raise any objections.

'It would serve her right if I didn't turn up,'

Jenny muttered to herself. 'But I suppose I might as well go. It's not as if I'm doing anything else and, after all, I did promise Mrs Ashcott I'd go and see her.'

When Alan phoned her later in the day to ask her if she would like to go to a skittles match with him on Saturday, she was quite glad she had a legitimate excuse for not going. He would only pester her to give him a definite answer to his proposal and she wanted more time to think it over, because she wasn't at all sure she loved him enough to marry him. She was fond of him, of course, and immensely attracted to him physically, but she knew this wasn't a sound enough basis for marriage. Perhaps they both needed to grow up a little first, so it was just as well she was going to St Cuthbert's in February. It would be time enough to make a final decision when she had finished her training.

'Baby-sitting for Doris Cottrell!' he exclaimed in disgust. 'Surely you can call it off? Then what about the afternoon? We could go for a drive or something.'

She explained she had promised to visit Mrs Ashcott and, after further argument, he arranged to give her a lift to the manor to save her having to wait for a bus.

'You might try to keep your week-ends free in future,' he grumbled, when he came to pick her up. 'I was counting on you coming to the match with me tonight.'

'Really, Alan,' she laughed. 'Don't look so badly done by. I'm sure you'll find somebody else without too much trouble.'

'That's not the point,' he retorted. 'I don't want just any girl to come along. I happen to want Jenny Clayton.' He leaned across to unhook her seat belt and, in doing so, he let his arm rest against her fractionally longer than was strictly necessary. 'You,' he whispered.

'I'll come with you next week,' she said a trifle breathlessly. 'I promise.'

'Then be sure you keep your promise,' he warned.

The manor gates were open so he was able to drive straight through, and he drew up with a flourish outside the brass-studded front door. 'Don't I get a kiss for my trouble?' he asked.

'Do behave, Alan,' she begged. 'Mrs Paget's probably watching.'

'Then we might as well give her something worth looking at,' he laughed, and he kissed her very thoroughly on the lips.

Somewhat ruffled she made her escape and, as she ran up the front steps, the door opened and Mrs Paget stood there, already dressed in her outdoor clothes. 'I was worried you wouldn't turn up on time,' she said, leading the way to the library. 'Another five minutes and I'd have missed my bus.'

'I understood Miss Ashcott would be here

till three o'clock,' Jenny remarked. 'I do think she might have waited till I arrived. Did she leave any messages for me?'

'Only that she'll be back before seven and would you see that Mrs Ashcott takes her medicine when she has her tea at four o'clock. I've put everything ready on a tray, so you'll only have to boil up a kettle, and I daresay you'll find your way around the kitchen. I'm sorry I can't stop, Miss, but there's not another bus for over an hour.'

'That's all right, Mrs Paget. Run along. And don't worry—I'll see to everything.'

Jenny spoke with more confidence than she felt because it was too bad of Gwen to have pushed off without leaving her full instructions. It reminded her of her first day on the wards when she hadn't a clue where anything was kept or what she was expected to do. But at least she had been able to ask one of the other nurses, whereas now she was on her own, and entirely responsible for an invalid who was unable to speak.

However, as it turned out, Mrs Ashcott was very little trouble. She still had the use of her left hand so she could, with difficulty, write short messages in a notebook. The fact that her hearing was unimpaired was also a great help and Jenny was able to bring her up to date with the village gossip, and she also read out extracts from the local paper which she had had the forethought to bring with her.

Shortly before going into the kitchen to get the tea she went over to the window to draw one of the curtains because the setting sun was shining full into Mrs Ashcott's eyes. The library was at the front of the house, so the french windows overlooked the full length of the drive, and she was surprised to see Alan's car was still parked outside the lodge.

He had told her he was 'Ma Pike's blue-eyed boy' and she supposed he must be filling in time with the Pikes before going to the skittles match. Then she remembered that Mr and Mrs Pike were away, visiting relatives, so Shirley must be the attraction. Well, why not? No doubt he was going to take her to the skittles match instead of Jenny. He had been quite open about getting somebody to take her place. But need they have stayed alone in the house all this time? And what were they doing to amuse themselves?

Disgusted with herself for thinking such sordid thoughts, Jenny tore herself away from the window and, having adjusted the cushion behind Mrs Ashcott's back, she said she was going to get the tea. 'How about some nice hot-buttered toast?' she asked. 'I can't think of anything nicer on a cold winter afternoon.'

After tea they watched the news on television and then they settled down to do a jigsaw puzzle. Morwenna had found these puzzles very therapeutic when she was recovering from her operation, and Jenny had borrowed one of the less complicated ones, a pleasant scene of an orchard in springtime. When the picture was completed Mrs Ashcott's glance strayed towards one of the bookshelves and, guessing what she wanted, Jenny fetched a book of A. E. Houseman's poetry and turned the pages till she came to the poem entitled 'A Shropshire Lad'. 'Loveliest of trees, the cherry now Is hung with bloom along the bough,' she read aloud in her gentle voice, and Mrs Ashcott leaned back in her chair and closed her eyes, with a look of peace on her face. Presently she slept and Jenny, who wasn't used to having time on her hands, passed the next hour very contentedly, reading the well-loved poems for her own enjoyment.

Gwen had the sense to arrive home just before seven o'clock, knowing full well she wouldn't be able to ask Jenny to help out again if she was late. 'I wish you'd let me pay you,' she said. 'You could be extremely useful to me, especially now that I know you're a trained nurse. Incidentally, I gather you covered yourself in glory the other night. Nigel was full of praise for the way in which you coped with the injured.'

'I only did what any other nurse would have done,' Jenny replied, and she said good-night to Mrs Ashcott and followed Crispin out to the car.

'Isn't Gwen marvellous the way she copes

with her mother?' the young man enthused. 'Most girls would put an invalid parent into a geriatric hospital.'

'The manor happens to belong to Mrs Ashcott and not to Gwen,' Jenny pointed out, 'and fortunately she has enough money to be able to afford the services of a private nurse so, when this has been arranged, she won't be putting Gwen to any inconvenience whatever. It seems to me that, even as things stand, Gwen has a whale of a time in comparison with what some daughters have to put up with.'

She felt annoyed with Crispin for allowing Gwen to pull the wool over his eyes, but no doubt he would shortly have a rude awakening. Crispin was the last person Gwen would be likely to marry and, although for the moment he was playing the part of her leading man, he was far too young for her, and she would have no hesitation in ditching him the moment she got her hooks into Nigel again.

CHAPTER EIGHT

Joe was already at the cottage when Jenny arrived and she was surprised he was so early, but Doris explained he had moved in as her lodger.

'I know what you're thinking,' she said, when Jenny went upstairs with her to see if

Harry and Benjy were asleep. 'But 'tisn't like that. I'm sleeping in with Linda and the little ones like I've always done. Cliff's got his room to himself and I've put Joe in Mum and Dad's room. He's not had any home life since his mother died and he'll be a lot more comfortable here than at Mrs Weaver's. That woman's a real old skinflint and he's been paying out good money to her all these months and getting next to nothing in return.'

'Wouldn't it be better if you and Joe got married?' Jenny suggested. 'It would put a stop to any gossip.'

'Reckon Joe wants to see what it's like living with all us lot before he lets me put the noose round his neck,' Doris answered. 'Can't say I blame him.' She tucked the bedclothes round the sleeping baby and, straightening up, she met Jenny's eye. 'Don't you worry about me, Miss. I can take care of myself. I'll cook and clean for Joe but that's as far as it'll go. If he wants anything else he'll have to wait till we're wed.'

Seeing the besotted look in Joe's eyes when they came downstairs, Jenny guessed that Doris's troubles would soon be sorted out. Fortunately she was a solid, homely girl, with her feet firmly planted on the ground and, even though Joe was sleeping under the same roof, he wouldn't be allowed a husband's privileges until everything was legal and binding. For her brothers' and sister's sake, as well as her own, Doris wanted security and she knew that, once she was wed, no one could take the children from her. Admittedly it was a sort of blackmail but, under the circumstances, Jenny didn't blame her, especially as she would certainly keep her side of the bargain and be a loving and considerate wife.

Tonight they were going to the pictures, and Jenny said her father was coming to pick her up soon after half-past ten but, if they were later, she would wait till they got back. As for Cliff, his leg was better and he was going to the Youth Club, so Jenny would be on her own with the younger children.

She played Snap and Halma with Linda until eight o'clock and then sent her off to bed, promising to come and kiss her good-night when she was ready to settle, but five minutes later the child came downstairs to tell her the rain was coming through the roof onto the landing, and Jenny had to fetch a bowl to catch the drips.

'I don't think the rain will ever stop,' Linda said in a voice full of foreboding. 'It'll be like the flood in the Bible and we'll have to bring all the animals indoors like Noah's ark. It's a bit scarey, isn't it, and I can't swim and neither can Benjy or Harry.'

'It would have to rain and rain for weeks and weeks for anything like that to happen,' Jenny said. 'In any case, you've forgotten about the rainbow and how God promised

He'd never flood the world again.'

Somewhat comforted Linda went back to bed and, having kissed her good-night, Jenny returned to the kitchen and got out her knitting. She hadn't done anything more to it since Cynthia's threatened miscarriage but, now that her friend was home from hospital, she felt encouraged to go ahead and knit a complete layette.

But she soon got bored and, in desperation, she fished out the record player and had another go at making it work. This time she was successful and, although 'Mr Wonderful' sounded more cracked than ever, he helped to pass the time very pleasantly until Joe and Doris got back from the pictures.

She told them about the leaking roof and Joe said he'd fix a new tile first thing in the morning but, when Jenny mentioned this to her father when he came to pick her up, he assured Doris the roof was the landlord's responsibility. 'Leave it to the experts,' he advised. 'If Joe starts messing around up there he'll probably make matters ten times worse and most likely fall off and break his neck into the bargain.'

'The Ashcotts own the cottage,' Jenny told him, 'but they haven't spent a penny on it for years.'

'Then it's about time they did.' Richard cast a critical glance at the damp patches on the walls and ceilings, the warped doors and ill-fitting window frames. 'It might be better if the whole place was pulled down and rebuilt.'

Doris looked daggers at him. 'Over my dead body,' she declared. 'I was born here and anyone who tries to pull it down will have me to reckon with.'

'She seems to think the wretched cottage should be preserved for posterity, like Shakespeare's birthplace,' Richard chuckled on the way home. 'I must say the girl's got character. When she marries Joe there's not much doubt as to who'll wear the breeches. I take it they're living together?'

Jenny shook her head. 'No, Dad,' she answered. 'Joe's the lodger.'

'Well, if Doris says he is it's probably true, but I wonder how many people will believe her. Not that it matters nowadays, more's the pity. Incidentally, you might let me know what happens about the roof. If nothing gets done I'll write the Ashcotts a letter pointing out their legal obligations.'

'That's nice of you, Dad, but I don't think you need bother. Nigel's promised to get Gwen to speak to her estate manager about it, so I'll jog his memory.'

Nothing more was said but, when Jenny saw Nigel on Monday morning, she told him about the leaking roof and how she had spent most of Saturday evening catching the drips.

'I didn't realize things were as bad as that,' he said. 'I'll certainly mention it to Gwen next time I see her, though I'm afraid Buckleigh will advise against any major repairs. The property simply isn't worth spending much money on.'

'Dad suggested it would be better to pull the whole place down and rebuild it, but you should have seen Doris's face.'

'I can well imagine, but it will have to come to that eventually—unless it falls down of its own accord, or gets swept away by floods.'

'That's what you're afraid of, isn't it?'

Nigel nodded. 'Yes, I am. With all this rain the situation is getting serious, but we can't force Doris to move if she doesn't want to. We'll just have to hope for the best. Meanwhile I don't see why she should put up with the inconvenience of a leaking roof. I'll call in and see Gwen some time today and tell her the matter is urgent.'

He kept his promise and, when he returned from his evening round, he waylaid Jenny just as she was getting ready to go home. 'Can you spare me a few minutes?' he asked. 'There's something I want to talk to you about.'

Rather intrigued—for the subject must surely be of more importance than the mending of Doris's roof—she followed him into the consulting-room. Doctor Hatherley was an inveterate muddler but she had spent a considerable amount of time tidying up after his evening surgery, and everything was commendably spick and span, but Nigel's mind was full of other matters and he only gave it a cursory glance. 'Sit down, Jenny,' he said. 'I want to talk to you about Mrs Ashcott, but first let me put your mind at rest with regard to the Cottrells' cottage. Gwen has promised to send round a builder tomorrow to do a patching up job on the roof, and Buckleigh will go with him and make a note of the necessary repairs, which will be seen to as soon as possible. She was most co-operative and, quite frankly, I can't think why Doris was afraid to ask for repairs to be done.'

Jenny guessed that Gwen's willing co-operation had been prompted by a desire to get into her ex-fiancé's good books. 'Doris's father always saw to everything himself,' she replied, 'and I should imagine it was from necessity rather than choice. Hasn't it occurred to you that, if Doris had done the asking instead of you, she would probably have met with a different response?'

Nigel raised an eyebrow but made no comment and Jenny wondered if he was annoyed with her for her implied criticism. She wished she knew for certain what his feelings were towards Gwen. He had been extremely angry with her for going to the point-to-point races and leaving her mother alone in the house, but that very same evening they had danced together in complete harmony, and nobody could deny they were a well-matched pair. 'You were going to talk to me about Mrs

Ashcott,' she reminded him.

'Yes, so I was. The situation is this—Gwen has interviewed several nurses, none of whom is willing to start work at the manor until after Christmas. I am naturally very concerned about Mrs Ashcott's welfare and I agree with Gwen that a visit by the district nurse only once a day isn't really sufficient.'

'I'm sure Gwen could cope if she really wanted to,' Jenny retorted. 'It's not as if Mrs Ashcott requires much in the way of skilled nursing.'

'I disagree. Not only does she require skilled nursing but she also needs constant attention, and she should never be left alone in the house, day or night.'

'All the same I would have thought that Gwen and Mrs Paget could work out a satisfactory rota between them, especially as Mrs Pike is willing to lend a hand if necessary. The trouble is Gwen's too selfish to give up any of her social engagements.'

Nigel shrugged. 'You may be right,' he agreed, 'but I believe that Mrs Ashcott herself would be much happier if a trained nurse was in attendance. To get to the point—I was wondering if you would consider taking over the job for the time being.'

Jenny stared at him in disbelief. 'What about my present job?' she demanded.

'You'll be leaving soon in any case,' he pointed out, 'and there's no reason why Carol shouldn't take over from you straightaway. You wouldn't lose out financially. The pay is excellent and it includes board and lodging. I would also think you would welcome the opportunity of doing some real nursing again before you go to Saint Cuthbert's. Most important of all, Mrs Ashcott has taken a fancy to you and you'll be doing her a real kindness if you agree to look after her until a more permanent arrangement can be made. A retired hospital nurse—a Miss Joyce Barraclough—seems to be the most promising of the applicants, and she will be free to come early in the New Year.'

Jenny was silent. It wasn't a decision she could make in a hurry, for, although she would be quite happy to look after Mrs Ashcott, she didn't relish the idea of living in the same house as Gwen. She also had misgivings about handing over her job to Carol, who always got her own way too easily.

While she was still hesitating the phone rang and Nigel picked up the receiver. Even from where she was sitting, Jenny could hear Gwen's voice, shrill and almost hysterical. 'I've just been talking to Jenny about it,' Nigel said soothingly. 'She's with me now and I'll hand you over to her.'

'Jenny? Is that you, Jenny?' Gwen sounded completely distraught. 'Look, I just can't stand it any longer. Mother's being frightfully difficult and Mrs Paget has just threatened to give in her notice. It's the last straw. If you won't come I'll have to put Mother into a nursing-home. I mean it, Jenny, I really do, even though Nigel says the move will probably kill her.'

It was blackmail, pure and simple, but Jenny had no defence against it. If she didn't agree to go Gwen would carry out her threat and poor Mrs Ashcott might well die of a broken heart. She had lived in the manor all her married life and she loved every stick and stone of it. Even if she was told the move was only temporary she would be desperately afraid she would never come home again.

'Very well. I'll come,' she agreed. 'How soon do you want me?'

'Tonight if possible. Tomorrow at the very latest.' Now that she had got her own way Gwen's voice resumed its normal pitch and Jenny suspected she had been putting on a big act. In an arrogant girl like Gwen, hysteria was quite out of character, but she and Carol were two of a kind and they would stop at nothing to gain their own ends.

Jenny put her hand over the receiver and looked questioningly at Nigel. 'Are you sure it will be all right by Doctor Hatherley?' she asked. 'I really should speak to him about it first.'

'I've already had a word with him,' Nigel replied. 'He says it's entirely up to you.'

'Then I might as well go this evening, as

soon as I've packed.' She spoke to Gwen again and then stood up. 'So this is good-bye.' She glanced round the consulting-room where she had so often in the past assisted Doctor Hatherley, and she experienced a momentary regret. It was true she would have been leaving soon, but this sudden departure wasn't giving her enough time to adjust. If she had stayed on till February, as she originally intended to do, she would have gone straight to Saint Cuthbert's to resume her chosen career. As it was, she was being bulldozed into taking a temporary job which didn't really appeal to her, because private nursing was often extremely boring and, inevitably, very lonely. Jenny enjoyed meeting people and she loved the busy, rewarding life working in a hospital. Never mind. It wouldn't be long before Miss Barraclough took over from her at the manor and, meanwhile, she would devote all her energies into making Mrs Ashcott as comfortable and happy as possible.

'I hope it won't be good-bye,' Nigel said as he walked with her to the door. 'I have persuaded Doctor Hatherley to let me take charge of Mrs Ashcott in future, so I shall be seeing you whenever I call at the manor, which will be quite frequently. Incidentally, I hope you'll let me drive you there this evening. How long will it take you to get ready? Shall we say nine o'clock? That should give you time to pack and have a bite to eat. Your parents and

Carol won't object to you being away from home at Christmas?'

'No, not a bit,' Jenny replied. 'They always spend Christmas with Wenna's brother and his family, who live up North, and they don't mind if I don't go with them. Actually, I've been away from home for the last two Christmasses.'

He smiled with relief. 'That's all right then. As a matter of fact, I don't think you'll find the festive season at all dull at the manor. Gwen's very party-minded and there should be plenty going on despite Mrs Ashcott's illness. Then, of course, there's the New Year's Eve ball, which is always a great occasion.'

'I doubt if Gwen will invite me to take part in the festivities,' Jenny said. 'I expect to be kept very much in the background.'

'Considering you're doing Gwen a favour, I'm sure she wouldn't have the nerve,' he declared but Jenny laughed and told him to wait and see.

Richard and Morwenna were rather dubious when she told them she was going to stay at the manor for a week or two to look after Mrs Ashcott, but Carol was over the moon at the prospect of taking over Jenny's job straightaway instead of having to wait until February. 'Good-oh!' she said. 'You've just about saved my bacon. Mummy's been awfully mean lately and she says I've got to manage on my allowance. She won't even give me an advance on my Christmas cheque. Goodness knows how she expects me to buy any decent presents.'

Jenny happened to know that Richard and Morwenna were giving Carol a car for Christmas, a far too generous gift which they tried to justify by saying it was a thank-offering for their daughter's return to health. Jenny wasn't particularly jealous but she thought it was a pity they couldn't get out of the habit of over-indulging their youngest child. 'You needn't have bought yourself that terriby pricey coat,' she pointed out. 'Alternatively you could have got yourself another temporary job.'

'I *did* try,' Carol pouted, 'but I couldn't find anything I liked. I kept hoping something decent would turn up.'

'Like a trip round the world with all expenses paid?' Jenny suggested sarcastically. 'Honestly, Carol, you're just about the limit.'

Her sister was quite unrepentant. 'Well, something did turn up, didn't it?' she chirruped. 'It nearly always does if you wish hard enough.'

'It's all right for some,' Jenny retorted, but she was smiling as she went upstairs to pack. She could never be cross with Carol for long but, all the same, it was going to be quite nice to have a short break away from home. Playing second fiddle to her sister was sometimes a little trying.

She had nearly finished packing when Morwenna came into the room with Jenny's newly ironed uniform. 'Are you sure you realize what you're letting yourself in for?' she asked, and there was a worried expression on her face. 'From all accounts Mrs Ashcott is a sweet lady, but Gwen is the last person on earth I'd want to work for.'

'It's only temporary, Wenna,' Jenny pointed out. 'If I don't go Mrs Ashcott will be put into a nursing-home over Christmas, which would be a dreadful thing to happen to the poor soul. I know she's had a severe stroke but she's still got all her faculties.'

'I must say I think it's extremely kind of you, but I'm afraid you'll be terribly lonely, cut off from all your friends, especially at Christmas,' Morwenna persisted.

'Not to worry. Nigel's promised to visit Mrs Ashcott every day, so he'll be my lifeline,' Jenny replied, but her cheerfulness was rather forced. It was all very well for Nigel to have taken over from Dr Hatherley as Mrs Ashcott's medical adviser, but this change of heart must mean he had overcome his aversion to meeting Gwen. In fact he was quite cheerfully making sure these meetings would become more and more frequent. Did this mean that, despite everything, he still found his ex-fiancée desirable? The thought disquieted her, and she wished with all her heart that she wasn't being forced into the rôle of unwilling onlooker. To see Nigel fall victim for a second time to Gwen's treacherous charm was too painful to contemplate and, if it had been humanly possible, she would have wriggled out of her commitment. But Gwen's mother needed her and she would be a poor nurse indeed if she ignored a plea for help. 'I'll stick it out for Mrs Ashcott's sake,' she told Morwenna, 'but Gwen had better watch her step because I certainly don't intend to be put upon.'

And, on this resolute note, she finished her packing, snapped her suitcase shut and went downstairs to wait for Nigel.

He picked her up punctually at nine o'clock and, when they arrived at the manor, Gwen answered the door herself. The warmth of her greeting was directed chiefly at Nigel, though she did condescend to smile at Jenny and remark that it was good of her to come at such short notice. She then called to Mrs Paget to show Jenny to her room. 'Mother sleeps downstairs, and the old butler's pantry has been made into a spare bedroom for you,' she said, speaking in the sort of voice she would use to a servant and, pointedly turning her back on Jenny, she put her arm in Nigel's and led him away to the library.

Inwardly seething, Jenny followed Mrs Paget, whose rather frosty manner softened as soon as they were alone. 'I'm right pleased to see you, Miss,' she admitted. 'Miss Ashcott would try the patience of a saint and I've only stayed on as long as this for Mrs Ashcott's sake.' She smoothed the bedspread and fiddled quite unnecessarily with the drawn curtains. 'I hope you'll find everything as you like it,' she continued. 'I've been sleeping down here myself to keep an eye on Mrs Ashcott at night, but I've given the room a good turn out and you won't find a speck of dust anywhere.'

'Thank you, Mrs Paget. It looks very nice.' Jenny humped her suitcase onto the bed and started to unpack. 'Can you give me a rough idea of what my duties will be?'

'There won't be much for you to do this evening, Miss. The district nurse came this morning and bathed and dressed Mrs Ashcott, and I've already undressed her and got her into bed. She's had her supper, but she'll be wanting a milky drink at ten, which I'll see to, and she'll settle soon afterwards. That's about all I can tell you, but the nurse will be coming first thing tomorrow morning and she'll give you full instructions before handing her patient over.'

'It sounds as if you all knew before I did that I was coming,' Jenny remarked. 'As a matter of fact Doctor Barrett only mentioned it to me a couple of hours ago.'

Mrs Paget rolled her eyes heavenwards. 'It's been brewing for days,' she confided. 'Ever since that bust-up last Wednesday when

Doctor Barrett tore Miss Ashcott a strip for leaving her mother alone in the house. She tried to put the blame on me but she knew full well I was catching the three o'clock bus, and she said it would be all right for me to go because she'd be back before four. It was the same last Saturday. Off she goes with Mr Crispin, not caring about the inconvenience to me, having to wait till you turned up, but luckily you got here in time and I caught the bus by the skin of my teeth. Sunday morning we had a real set-to. The mess she'd left in the kitchen for me to clear up you wouldn't believe. Burnt saucepans all over the place and, to crown all, the cat had been sick through being given chicken bones, and she hadn't done a thing about it. I tell you, the smell turned my stomach. For two pins I'd have packed my bags and left but I knew she'd put her mother in a nursing-home if I did. To cut a long story short she could see I'd come to the end of my tether and she got down off her high horse and begged me to stay on and she said she was going to fix up with Doctor Barrett for you to come and look after Mrs Ashcott. I hope it's a permanent arrangement, Miss. I can see you and me are going to get along together, but I've lived in some houses where there's been a private nurse and you wouldn't believe the airs and graces they put on.'

Jenny shook her head. 'I'm only filling in

over the holiday period,' she explained. 'I shall be leaving as soon as Miss Barraclough comes.'

'I'm sorry to hear that, Miss. Well, I shall just have to wait and see. This was a nice job in the old days, when Mrs Ashcott was in good health but, the way things are, I don't see much future in it.'

'Then you used to work for the Ashcotts before they went to Canada?' Jenny hesitated. 'So you know Gwen was once engaged to Doctor Barrett?'

Mrs Paget nodded. 'I was with the Ashcotts for five years,' she answered, 'and I know all about the way Miss Gwen treated Doctor Barrett. Between you and me, I can't understand why he's taking up with her again. Once bitten, twice shy I'd have thought, but it doesn't seem to be like that and I wouldn't be surprised if she gets his ring back on her finger again. She's clever, is Miss Gwen, I'll say that for her, but, if Doctor Barrett marries her, he'll live to rue the day. Oh well, I mustn't stand here gossiping. I'll leave you to your unpacking and, if there's anything you need, you've only to say the word.'

Jenny spent some time arranging the room to her liking, then she looked in on Mrs Ashcott but she was peacefully dozing so she didn't disturb her. Instead, she went in search of Gwen because there were several matters she wished to discuss with her, and she naturally assumed that Nigel would have left long since. However, when she went into the library he was still there, looking very much at home in one of the comfortable armchairs, his long legs stretched out in front of the fire, while Gwen was seated opposite him, smoking a cigarette.

'Yes, Jenny? Did you want something?' she asked, glancing briefly over her shoulder. 'Can't it wait till later?'

'I'm sorry,' Jenny said, cross with herself for apologizing. 'I didn't realize Nigel was still here.'

'I was just going,' he replied imperturbably. He had risen from his chair when Jenny came into the room and Gwen was forced to do likewise. 'I was only waiting to say good-bye.'

'Honestly, Nigel, that's not very gall*an*t of you.' Gwen stressed the last syllable in the way that always irritated Jenny. She had the habit, too, of making witty asides, which also irritated her. In fact there were very few things about Gwen that didn't irritate her.

'I wouldn't have stopped to unpack if I'd realized you were waiting,' she said, looking directly at Nigel.

'Shouldn't you be sitting with Mother?' Gwen interrupted.

'That was one of the things I wanted to talk to you about,' Jenny replied. 'I haven't a clue what is expected of me, what sort of duties I have and what free time, so perhaps we could discuss it when we're alone. Good-night, Nigel, and thanks for the lift.'

'I'll see myself out,' he said, effectively squashing any attempt on Gwen's part to speed him on his way. 'It's extremely kind of you, Jenny, to take over at such short notice and I'm sure Mrs Ashcott will be most appreciative.'

'I hope I shan't let you down,' Jenny replied. 'I'm very out of practice.'

'Skills once learnt aren't easily forgotten,' he reminded her. 'I think you proved your mettle to everyone's satisfaction the other night.'

He spoke with such warmth that Gwen looked more put out than ever. 'I'm afraid you're going to miss your clever little receptionist,' she said acidly, 'but it will be nice for her to see how the other half lives.' She bestowed a superior smile on Jenny. 'There have been Ashcotts living at the manor since the time of Richard the Lionheart. History has it that Arabella Ashcott was the King's mistress.'

Jenny kept a perfectly straight face. 'I daresay my ancestors slept around a bit too,' she retorted, 'but I don't brag about it.'

Gwen looked daggers at her and Nigel tactfully hid a chuckle behind a cough. He had been a shade apprehensive about introducing Jenny into the Ashcott household but fortunately she had plenty of spunk and, from the look of things, she was perfectly capable of holding her own.

During the following week Jenny kept out of Gwen's way as much as possible and they rarely met, even at mealtimes, because Gwen invariably had her breakfast in bed, was often out to lunch, and she spent several evenings a week rehearsing with the Plumpton Players. This suited Jenny very well and she spent most of her time with Mrs Ashcott, being a companion to her as well as a nurse.

It was a boring rather than an arduous job and she fretted at her forced inactivity, for she was an energetic girl who liked getting out and about and meeting people. This may have been partly why she found herself looking forward so much to Nigel's daily visit—she brought with him a breath of the outside world, and she enjoyed hearing the snippets of news he imparted. Carol was pulling her weight, Mrs Bond's baby was doing fine, the victims of the car crash were all making excellent progress, and Doris's roof had been mended. She likened it to tuning in to her favourite radio programme, which made a welcome break to the tedium of the long day, and she found herself listening with eager anticipation for the sound of his car. He usually arranged to call around teatime and it became almost a social occasion, causing the deepest disappointment both to herself and Mrs Ashcott if four o'clock came and there was no ring at the front door bell.

Gwen was usually out in the afternoon but, a few days before Christmas, she happened to come home just as Nigel was leaving. Jenny was crossing the hall with him when Gwen came in through the front door, her arms laden with holly and mistletoe, and her vibrant dark hair escaping from her scarlet woollen hat.

Holding aloft a sprig of mistletoe she laughingly invited Nigel to give her a kiss, while Jenny hung back, miserably conscious of being at a disadvantage. Dressed in her uniform she was sure she looked decidedly frumpish in comparison with Gwen, whose dashing scarlet cloak and black knee-length boots were the height of fashion. Not very surprisingly Nigel accepted the invitation with apparent alacrity, and he stepped forward and gave Gwen a casual kiss, at the same time plucking a single berry from the bough. She returned his kiss with unnecessary warmth.

'Happy Christmas, darling,' she said, dropping her parcels on the floor and flinging her arms round his neck. 'Can you stay and help me decorate?'

'I'm afraid not. Duty calls,' he replied, but Jenny fancied that his eyes rested admiringly on the laughing girl, and that he was genuinely sorry he couldn't linger.

'Too bad,' Gwen pouted. 'You're always too busy nowadays to have fun. But surely you'll have time off over Christmas? I was going to phone you and ask you to come to dinner on Christmas Eve. Quite a small dinner party. You and me—and Jenny, of course,' she added as an afterthought. 'And I'll invite Crispin to make up a foursome. Do say you'll come.'

'Yes, I'd like to very much,' he answered and, with a brief nod in Jenny's direction, he took his leave.

Jenny found herself looking forward to Christmas Eve with mixed feelings. Her first thought had been—what should she wear? She had brought nothing suitable with her and, in any case, her very nicest dress had been ruined on the night of the accident when she had helped Nigel attend to the unfortunate victims, and she would have no opportunity to go shopping for a replacement. Eventually she decided to phone Richard and ask him to bring along a pale blue, sleeveless dress she had bought last summer. Morwenna would pack it up for her and she could be trusted to include suitable accessories.

However, on the very day of the dinner party she had a pleasant surprise. A delivery van arrived at the manor soon after breakfast, with a parcel addressed to her, and inside was the prettiest dress she had ever seen, and a note from the girl who had been injured in the car crash, telling her the name of the shop where the dress had been purchased, and saying it could be changed if it wasn't suitable.

'A small token of thanks for a debt that can never be repaid—I do hope you will like it,' ran the note. 'I felt dreadful when I saw your dress was spoilt and I'm afraid your evening was spoilt as well.' It was signed 'Victoria Hobson' and there was a PS 'I got your size from Doctor Barrett, and your present address—wasn't it kind of him to come and visit me in hospital?'

The letter was an odd mixture of the formal and the informal, and Jenny decided that the writer was a girl whose life had been well worth saving, though she was doubtful if her drunken companion was an equally deserving case.

She tried on the dress, which fitted perfectly, and then went into Mrs Ashcott's room to show it to her and explain where it had come from. Mrs Ashcott nodded approvingly and, pointing to the dressing-table, she indicated that she wanted her jewel case brought over to the bed. Jenny opened it for her, and exclaimed with delight when Mrs Ashcott lifted out a jade necklace and handed it to her to put on.

'It's beautiful,' she breathed. 'May I really borrow it?'

In sign language Mrs Ashcott indicated that it was a gift and she reached up a trembling hand and patted Jenny on the cheek, the look of affection in her eyes speaking as clearly as any words could have done. Jenny felt moved to tears and, leaning forward, she kissed Mrs Ashcott with genuine affection, wondering how it was possible for a mother and daughter to be such poles apart.

Gwen had invited Nigel and Crispin to come at seven o'clock, and Mrs Paget promised to keep an eye on Mrs Ashcott so that Jenny would be free to enjoy her first evening of leisure since coming to the manor.

Jenny stayed in the kitchen until nearly half-past six, helping Mrs Paget with the cooking and other preparations, and then she hurried into her bedroom to change out of her nurse's uniform into the lovely evening gown presented to her by Victoria Hobson. She had no idea what Gwen was going to wear and she experienced a moment's misgiving, wondering if the dress was too formal for the occasion, but it was too late now to change her mind. She realized she had been rather foolish to leave herself so little time to get ready, but Mrs Paget was in a fluster and it had seemed mean to leave her to get on with all the preparations on her own, because naturally Gwen would never dream of helping.

Gwen had spent the afternoon at the hairdresser and she had arrived home looking even more glamorous than usual, while for the past hour she had been closeted in the bathroom, making herself look even more delectable than nature had intended. Certainly Jenny couldn't compete with her, though a hurried look in the dressing-table mirror assured her that she didn't look at all bad—thanks to the new dress and to the fact that her hair never needed much attention, being naturally full of bounce and highlights. All she ever did was to wash it herself and set it in a few large rollers, and this she had done while Mrs Ashcott was resting after lunch.

The menfolk were a few minutes late arriving which gave Gwen an opportunity to speak to Jenny. 'What a pretty frock,' she said with deceptive friendliness. 'Perhaps a little over—or should I say *under* dressed for the occasion?' She herself was wearing an expensive cocktail suit—slinky black trousers tapered at the ankle, and a black lace tabard, high-necked and long-sleeved, yet revealing more than it concealed. Her eyes narrowed as she looked at the necklace circling Jenny's slim neck. 'So Mother has lent you the jade necklace,' she remarked. 'I hope you'll take care of it. It's a family heirloom and worth quite a lot of money.'

'It was a gift from your mother,' Jenny replied, 'but I had no idea it was valuable, so of course I'll return it.'

'Yes, please do. I daresay Mother will shower you with presents if you give her half a chance, so you might be tactful and let me have them back on the quiet. They are mostly collectors' pieces, you know.'

'You needn't worry,' Jenny retorted with

spirit. 'The last thing I want to do is rob you.'

'In that case, would you kindly keep off the grass where Nigel is concerned?' Gwen's mask had slipped and she no longer made any attempt to disguise her feelings of animosity. 'He happens to be my property and I don't intend to let him slip through my fingers again. If you're desperate for a man you can have Crispin—he's served his purpose, so I've no further use for him.' She spoke with an insolent arrogance which made Jenny's blood boil but, before she could think of a suitable reply, the front door bell rang and Crispin came in, followed a few minutes later by Nigel.

Watching him as he greeted Gwen, a feeling of desolation swept over Jenny, for, despite the fact that he was no longer blind to his ex-fiancée's faults, it was abundantly clear that he still found her breathtakingly attractive. Yes, even though he had broken away from her once, he was still inescapably bound to her. Jenny recalled the look in his eyes when Gwen had burst unannounced into the consulting-room, his anger melting like snow in summer sunshine. The kiss under the mistletoe, brief but full of promise. Ah yes, the bonds were still there and this time Gwen would make no mistake. She was older and wiser than she had been a year ago, and she would be careful not to wound his pride a second time by playing fast and loose with other suitors.

The evening Jenny had been looking

forward to with so much eager anticipation turned out to be an ordeal. Gwen monopolized Nigel, and Crispin was forced to give most of his attention to Jenny who felt so sorry for him she responded with more warmth than she realized. Occasionally she caught Nigel's rather puzzled glance and her colour would rise. But pride would come to her rescue and she would turn again to Crispin with a laughing remark, successfully bridging the momentary silence.

When the meal was over they went into the library for coffee and immediately afterwards Gwen turned to Nigel. 'Mother would like to see you before she settles for the night,' she said, linking her arm in his. 'You can put on the record player, Jenny,' she added, 'unless you can find something better to do.'

The implication behind her words was so clear that Jenny flushed with embarrassment and she was afraid that, for politeness sake, Crispin would feel impelled to make a pass at her. Murmuring a hurried excuse about having to fetch a handkerchief, she escaped to her bedroom where she remained hiding for nearly fifteen minutes, by which time she was sure Gwen and Nigel would have returned to the library. However, when she opened her door, she was appalled to see them only just emerging from Mrs Ashcott's bedroom.

She stood frozen as they crossed the hall but, instead of going into the library, Gwen paused and gave Nigel a provocative look. She was evidently teasing him about the brevity of his kiss under the mistletoe. 'We haven't an audience now,' she reminded him, 'and do we really need mistletoe? In the old days kissing was in favour whatever the season.'

His reply was inaudible but there was no mistaking the force with which he pulled her into his arms and the passionate ardour with which he kissed her, though had Jenny remained a spectator for a moment longer, she would have seen him push the girl angrily away from him, ashamed of his momentary weakness. 'I didn't come here tonight with the intention of making love to you,' he said. 'The old days are long past and, as far as I'm concerned, kissing is definitely out of season. In any case, I think it's time we joined the others.' And, with an air of finality, he opened the library door and stood aside to let her pass.

Jenny would have given anything to have been able to stay in her bedroom for the rest of the evening, but she knew her non-appearance would give rise to speculation so, as soon as she had regained control of her emotions, she made herself rejoin the others in the library.

'Ah, there you are!' Gwen exclaimed. 'Crispin has just been suggesting we go out carol singing. Don't you think that's a good idea? I hope you're in good voice tonight. Crispin's a tenor, Nigel's a baritone and I'm a contralto, so we could do with a soprano. We thought we'd drive over to Bob and Jean's and pick up the rest of the Plumpton crowd on our way. Could be fun.'

Without waiting for a reply she dashed out of the room, leaving Jenny in a state of indecision. From what she had seen of the 'Plumpton crowd' she wasn't all that keen on them, but both Nigel and Crispin seemed to take it for granted that she would be coming with them, and they would think it extremely odd if she backed out. 'I'll have a word with Mrs Paget,' she said. 'I daresay it will be all right for me to come with you, but I'll have to be back reasonably early, as I know she wants to go to Midnight Mass.'

Fortunately Mrs Paget was quite willing to hold the fort for a couple of hours and, when Jenny was ready, she looked in on Mrs Ashcott in order to satisfy herself that all was well with her patient. It had been a dull evening for the poor invalid, who had been bundled off to bed considerably earlier than usual, but she seemed perfectly content and greeted Jenny with her customary serene smile.

'We're going out carol singing,' Jenny told her. 'I won't be late back but Mrs Paget will bring you your milk at ten o'clock and settle you for the night.' She lingered for a few minutes, to plump up the pillows and check the contents of the bedside table. Then she kissed Mrs Ashcott good-night and went into the kitchen to say good-bye to Mrs Paget. By this time Gwen and Crispin had already left, and Nigel was waiting for her in the library.

'We'll drive over to Bob and Jean's,' he said, 'and I can leave the car there while we go carol singing. Everyone's sure to go back afterwards and stay till the small hours but I promise to drive you home at a reasonable time.'

'Oh dear! Isn't that a nuisance for you? I don't want to drag you away from the party,' Jenny objected.

'Don't worry about that,' he replied. 'I'm not particularly enamoured with the Plumpton Players and, in any case, I've got to get back to the surgery in case there are any night calls. I promised Doctor Hatherley I wouldn't be much later than eleven o'clock.'

'Are you spending Christmas day with the Wickhams?' she asked a trifle wistfully as they got into the car. 'I wish I could come too. It's ages since I last went to the farm and I'm longing to see Sweet Briar again.'

His mouth tightened. 'Is it Sweet Briar or Alan who is main attraction?' he asked with an abrupt change of mood. 'I wish you'd get over your infatuation for my good-for-nothing cousin.'

Jenny was already a trifle overwrought and the uncalled for remark made her see red. 'I don't know why you always insist on calling Alan "good-for-nothing",' she retorted. 'He's hoping to get the managership of the Ashcott estate and, if you ask me, he'll make a much better job of it than Mr Buckleigh does. Look at the way the Cottrells' cottage was allowed to go to rack and ruin till you stepped in and made Gwen do something about it. It's probably the same all over the estate.'

Nigel was somewhat taken aback by the forcefulness of her reply but he failed to read the danger signals. 'I'm sorry but I can't see Alan pulling his weight wherever he works,' he declared. 'He's always been bone lazy.'

Jenny's eyes flashed. 'That's only because of the way Cynthia treats him,' she insisted. 'She ought to make him a partner instead of just putting him on the payroll. I don't suppose he earns much more than an ordinary farm hand.'

'Is that what he told you?' Nigel gave a short laugh. 'I happen to know he has a very generous allowance—far more than he deserves. My uncle knew what he was doing when he left the farm to Cynthia instead of Alan. If my good-for-nothing cousin had inherited he would have gambled it away in less than a year.'

At any other time Jenny might have taken notice of what he said, but she was so outraged by the scene she had just witnessed between him and Gwen, that she was in the mood to prefer an out-and-out flirt to a man who was so weak that he allowed himself to make love to the very girl who in the past had cheated and humiliated him.

'You're always running him down,' she flared. 'At least he isn't stuffy and self-opinionated like some people I could name. I like Alan. He's fun to be with and *he* doesn't pretend to be a saint.'

Nigel caught hold of her wrist in a vice-like grip. 'I think you had better explain what you mean,' he said angrily.

'Do I have to?' she retorted. 'I would have thought it was only too obvious.' Tearing herself out of his grasp, she opened the car door and stumbled out. 'I'm not coming carol singing with you,' she said. 'You can make what excuses you like to the others. Good-*night*.' And, slamming the car door shut, she turned and ran back up the drive, leaving him staring after her with a puzzled expression on his face.

He waited until she disappeared inside the house. Then he drove slowly away in the direction of the surgery. Bob and Jean and the rest of the Plumpton crowd would have to manage as best they could without the help of his pleasant baritone voice because he, too, had suddenly lost all desire to go carol singing.

CHAPTER NINE

Mrs Paget had been given extra time off over Christmas to stay with her married daughter, which meant that Jenny had been completely housebound for several days. The housekeeper remarked that she was looking rather peaky and suggested she might like to take the whole afternoon off and go riding.

'But it's Wednesday,' Jenny objected. 'You usually catch the three o'clock bus and go to your daughter.'

'I'll catch the five o'clock instead. She's taking me to a concert this evening, or I'd give it a miss altogether. Strikes me Miss Gwen will have to mend her ways and stay at home a lot more often when Miss Barraclough comes. *She* won't put up with the sort of hours you've been expected to work.'

Jenny shrugged. 'I haven't minded,' she said. 'Mrs Ashcott's a wonderful lady, so sweet and understanding, and I've become really fond of her. All the same I'll be glad of a break, so, if you're sure you don't mind . . .?'

Mrs Paget gave her a friendly push. 'You'd best get off as early as possible, while the sun's still shining,' she advised. 'I was listening to the weather forecast and there's more rain on the way.'

Jenny hadn't seen Cynthia since her

threatened miscarriage, and she hadn't exercised Sweet Briar for ages, so she felt quite excited at the prospect of spending the afternoon at the Wickhams' farm. She phoned Cynthia but unfortunately she was going to the clinic with Guy for a check-up. 'But please come all the same,' her friend persuaded her. 'Sweet Briar could do with some exercise. Cliff's supposed to ride her every day, but he's got to help Alan with the hedging this afternoon, so he won't be able to spare the time.'

It was a two-mile walk from the manor to the farm but this didn't worry Jenny. She loved the country and she found it far more interesting than the town, even in Winter when the trees were bare. Arriving at the farm she went straight to the stables and, having saddled Sweet Briar, she set off at an easy canter over the downs.

Facing into the sun, she didn't notice the heavy storm clouds gathering behind her, and the sudden onslaught of torrential rain took her by surprise. Putting up the hood of her anorak she rode on for a little while, hoping the rain would ease off, but it was soon apparent that it had set in for the rest of the afternoon, and she decided it was pointless to go any further.

The quickest way back to the farm was via the bridge about a mile down-river from the Cottrells' cottage. She paused half-way across to look down at the swirling waters and she could hardly believe she had crossed over by stepping stones only a few weeks ago. Following a week of rain the shallow water had turned into a raging torrent, but the banks were high on either side, and the bridge had been strongly built to withstand the worst of the winter storms. If it hadn't been for what Nigel had said it would never have struck her that the people who lived in the valley —and particularly the Cottrells—were vulnerable to flooding. Even now she thought he was exaggerating the danger, because the authorities would have checked up carefully before allowing the owners of the new paint factory to divert a half-mile stretch of the river.

Back at the farm she gave Sweet Briar a brisk rub down before going into the house to dry herself off. She felt she couldn't face a two-mile walk in the pouring rain: it would be more sensible to wait till Guy and Cynthia returned and then ask Guy to give her a lift back to the manor. They should be home well before four o'clock and, as Mrs Paget wasn't leaving till just before five, she would be back in plenty of time.

Not wishing to be idle she looked around for something to do and, finding a big pile of ironing, she got out the ironing-board and set to work but, by a quarter past four, she was beginning to feel distinctly uneasy. Surely they should have returned by now? She didn't know what to do because, even if she braved the rain, she couldn't possibly be home in time for the housekeeper to catch her bus.

In the end she decided to phone through to the manor and explain the situation. After all, it wouldn't be the end of the world if Mrs Paget missed the concert. She would make it up to her somehow, and there was probably something on television she would be quite happy to watch instead.

But it was Gwen and not Mrs Paget who answered the phone, and she listened rather icily to Jenny's excuses. 'You should have come straight back instead of waiting around for a lift,' she said. 'I hope you realize you are putting me to considerable inconvenience. Mrs Paget's son-in-law came to pick her up because the weather was so awful, and I had to let her go or she'd have raised the roof, so I'm stuck here until you condescend to come home.'

'I've said I'm sorry,' Jenny retorted, 'though it's a bit unreasonable of you to kick up such a fuss. It's not as if you'll have to do anything for your mother. Mrs Paget promised to give her her tea before she left and she'll be quite happy sitting watching television. I'll come home as soon as Guy and Cynthia get back.'

Gwen replaced the receiver without deigning to reply, leaving Jenny to reflect indignantly that the more one does the more one is expected to do. It wasn't even as if it was a job she had particularly wanted, and she had only agreed to take it for Mrs Ashcott's sake.

Thank heaven it was only a temporary arrangement. She would be more than pleased to hand over to Miss Barraclough—and the best of British luck to the poor woman. She'd have to be either a saint or a fool to put up with Gwen's inconsiderate ways.

Shortly after five o'clock Alan came in, wet through and not in the best of tempers, but he cheered up when he saw Jenny. 'Hullo there,' he said. 'So you've come out of hiding at last.' He had phoned her several times during the past week, hoping to fix a date with her, but without success, and he was beginning to think she was deliberately avoiding him. 'You might have told me you were coming,' he grumbled. 'I'd have given the hedging a miss and we could have spent the afternoon together.'

'I didn't know I was going to get time off until the last minute,' she explained. 'You surely haven't been working outdoors in all this rain? You're wet through.' She took his sodden coat and hung it over the back of a chair.

'We sheltered for some of the time in the shepherd's house,' he replied, 'but when the rain showed no sign of easing off I sent Cliff home and decided to call it a day. It was a mug's game trying to get the hedging done in this weather, but my tyrannical brother-in-law works to the calendar—hedging this week, potato riddling next week, then the ditching and muck-spreading, and if you don't like the weather you can lump it.'

'I thought those jobs were done by the farmhands,' Jenny remarked.

Alan shrugged. 'Labour's expensive nowadays and we do a lot of the work ourselves.' He pulled a long face, but Jenny rightfully suspected he was painting an exaggerated picture for her benefit. 'Can you rustle me up a meal while I go and change out of my wet things?' he asked. 'Cynthia and Guy won't be back till late and I'm famished.'

Jenny stared at him in dismay. 'I thought they were only going to the clinic,' she said. 'I've been waiting around, hoping for a lift home.'

'They're spending the evening with Guy's parents,' Alan explained. 'But don't worry. I'll drive you home when I've had something to eat.'

By the time he came downstairs she had cooked a plateful of eggs and bacon for him and, while he ate, she told him how important it was for her to get back to the manor without delay. 'Gwen sounded very annoyed on the phone,' she said. 'She's probably waiting to go out to a rehearsal.'

'You ought to stand up for your rights,' he said, with a careless laugh. 'Let her wait. It will do her good.'

'It's Mrs Ashcott I'm concerned about. If Gwen goes out and leaves her alone in the house anything might happen, and I would be held responsible.'

'I refuse to budge for at least an hour,' he declared. 'I don't see why I should get indigestion to please Gwen. Relax, darling. You take your duties too seriously.'

Jenny tried to persuade herself that he was probably right. After all, what could possibly happen during her absence? It wasn't as if Mrs Ashcott would be on her own because, although Gwen had made out she was being put to considerable inconvenience, it was hardly likely she would want to go out before seven o'clock at the earliest, and it was now only just after half-past five.

But Jenny still felt uneasy and she wished Alan would get a move on but, even after he had finished his meal, he made no attempt to hurry.

'How about another cup of tea?' he asked. It suited him to have Jenny fetch and carry for him, to cook his meal and dry his coat in front of the Aga stove. It was a foretaste of what life would be like when they were married and living in the estate manager's house on the Ashcott estate. 'This is nice, isn't it?' he said persuasively. 'Just you and me together, snug and warm, with the rain beating on the window. Surely you can stay a little longer?' He got up from his chair and pulled her up to stand beside him. 'I love you, Jenny,' he whispered. 'You're the only girl I've ever cared for.'

She tried to push him away, remembering the last time this had happened, and how nearly she had given in to his demands, but his mouth sought hers and he kissed her with passionate ardour. 'When are you going to give me an answer?' he demanded. 'You've had ten days grace already, and you can't keep me dangling on a string for ever.'

'But, Alan I'm still not sure,' she faltered. 'Everything's all right when you hold me in your arms like this, but there's more to marriage than kissing and cuddling. I must have more time to think about it.'

He held her away from him, his face dark with anger. 'I'm no saint, Jenny,' he said forcefully. 'If I can't have you, then I'll have some other girl. But it's you I want. For God's sake, don't turn me down. If you marry me I swear I'll make a model husband.'

He kissed her again, even more passionately than before and she was struggling desperately to free herself when the kitchen door opened and Nigel strode in.

He came to a halt just inside the door and the repressed anger in his voice made Jenny wince. 'I beg your pardon,' he said contemptuously. 'I seem to be intruding.'

'You certainly are,' Alan retorted. 'You might at least have had the politeness to knock on the door before bursting in on us. What the devil do you want?'

Nigel ignored him, and his ice-cold glance

rested on Jenny. 'Get your coat,' he ordered. 'It may interest you to know that Mrs Ashcott has had a fall. Fortunately no bones are broken but she's badly shocked.'

Jenny gasped, distressed not only by this disquieting news but also by his belligerent attitude.

'Don't speak to Jenny like that,' Alan interrupted. 'Who do you think you are, ordering her about in that lofty manner?'

'I happen to be Mrs Ashcott's medical adviser,' Nigel replied. 'Jenny knows very well she is at fault. She should have been back on duty hours ago.' Without another glance at either of them he strode out to the car, leaving Jenny to grab her coat and follow almost at a run.

'I couldn't get away before,' she stammered. 'I was waiting for Guy to drive me home.'

'Why not Alan?' he enquired in icy tones.

'He's only been home a short time,' she answered, fully aware that it sounded a feeble excuse. 'He was wet through and wanted a meal.'

'You should get your priorities right,' he remarked cuttingly. 'You appear to have forgotten that a good nurse always puts her patients first. Fortunately Gwen was at home when it happened or the results might have been tragic. I really cannot understand how you could be so inconsiderate and selfish. Gwen expected you home before dark and, when you didn't turn up, she had to cancel an important engagement.'

'I phoned to say I'd be late,' Jenny said, almost in tears.

He raised an eyebrow. 'Was it necessary to be as late as this?' he remarked. 'Or do you consider your own pleasure takes precedence over everything else?' He gave vent to his feelings by stepping hard on the accelerator, causing the car to shoot forward at an alarming speed, and Jenny cried out as they narrowly missed an oncoming vehicle. It was unlike Nigel to be so careless and she stole an anxious glance at his set face, noticing that his hands were tightly clenched on the steering-wheel.

'Must you go so fast?' she asked in a trembling voice. She hadn't seen him since their quarrel on Christmas Eve and evidently the interval between had done little to sweeten his temper.

'I have a couple of urgent calls to make,' he answered, making no attempt to slow down. 'Gwen phoned me at the surgery just as I was leaving, so it was an unforeseen delay and I can't waste precious time listening to excuses.'

He turned the car into the drive and, bringing it to a screeching standstill, he leapt out. 'Come along—don't just sit there,' he said as she fumbled miserably with the door handle. 'I happen to be in a hurry.' He jerked the door open for her and impatiently waited while she got out.

'Please, Nigel,' she pleaded. 'Let me explain.'

'Further explanations are quite unnecessary,' he answered with an air of finality. 'You surely don't expect me to disbelieve the evidence of my own eyes?'

Hearing the car, Gwen had already opened the front door. 'Nigel, darling, I don't know how to thank you,' she purred. 'I'm afraid your evening has been completely disrupted.' She turned to Jenny. 'I can't think what you've been up to all this time,' she said in a completely different tone of voice. 'You'd better go straight in to Mother and make her comfortable. She's very restless and probably needs a sedative or something.' And then, even before Jenny was out of earshot, she turned back to Nigel. 'I hope you tore her off a strip for neglecting her duties,' she said vindictively. '. . . Yes, she did ring up but it wasn't until after Mrs Paget left, so it was incredibly lucky that I happened to come home when I did. For all Jenny cared Mother could have been alone in the house for hours.'

Jenny could hardly believe her ears. Gwen was deliberately twisting the truth in order to make it sound as if Jenny had been negligent, and she was doing it so cleverly that it would be impossible for her to defend herself. Whatever she said Nigel would disbelieve her.

She turned blindly away, an unbearable pain

tearing at her heart. What a disastrous outing it had been. First the rainstorm which had driven her into the farm to shelter. Cynthia and Guy not coming straight home from the clinic. Alan's unwelcome attentions. And then, the final blow. Nigel turning up and witnessing what must have appeared to be a passionate love scene between herself and Alan. How could fate have been so cruel?

But there was no time for self-pity. Fighting back her tears she put on her uniform and, composing herself as best she could, she went hurriedly into Mrs Ashcott's bedroom. As Nigel so rightly said—she must get her priorities right. The needs of her patient must come first and she would be a poor nurse indeed if she allowed her personal feelings to take precedence.

Mrs Ashcott passed a peaceful night and the next morning she seemed none the worse for her fall, but Jenny had been so concerned about her she had spent the night on a camp bed in the same room, sleeping only fitfully and getting up at hourly intervals to make sure her patient hadn't contracted bronchial pneumonia. During her nursing career she had seen many sick people die as the result of a fall and she would never forgive herself if the same thing happened to Mrs Ashcott.

She felt tired and listless but she knew this was due more to the scene she had had with Nigel the previous evening than to her broken night. Remembering the scornful look in his eyes when he burst into the farm kitchen and found her in Alan's arms, she gulped back a sob. Surely he needn't have been so angry with her? It was Gwen's fault, not hers, that Mrs Ashcott had fallen and it was unfair of him to lay the blame on her.

As she went about her duties she found herself dreading her next meeting with him, and even Gwen remarked on her haggard appearance. 'My dear girl,' she said, in her pseudo friendly way. 'You look like death warmed up. Didn't you get any sleep last night?'

'Very little,' Jenny admitted. 'I was worried about your mother. It always gives cause for concern when an invalid has a fall.'

'Yes, I know—that's why I sent for Nigel straightaway.' Butter wouldn't have melted in Gwen's mouth. 'I could see she hadn't broken any bones, but I thought I'd better be on the safe side.'

All Jenny's pent-up resentment came to the surface. 'You mean you wanted an excuse to tell tales about me,' she retorted. 'Well, I hope you're satisfied. Nigel's convinced it was my fault but you know perfectly well I phoned long before Mrs Paget was due to leave, and she wouldn't have gone off early if you hadn't been at home to look after your mother.'

Gwen raised her delicately plucked eyebrows. 'I don't know what you're talking about,' she replied. 'I merely told Nigel you'd gone to the Wickhams for the afternoon and, as you didn't seem to be in any hurry to come home, he very kindly offered to fetch you.'

'You made it sound as if I was in the wrong,' Jenny argued. 'Half truths are often more damaging than a downright lie.'

Gwen gave an amused laugh. 'What a carry on,' she remarked. 'And all because you have taken a tumble in Nigel's estimation. I can't see why his good opinion of you matters one way or the other—it's not as if you'll be seeing much of him in the future. I believe you're starting work at Saint Cuthbert's in February and, when Nigel and I are married, I very much doubt if you'll be on our visiting list.'

The colour drained from Jenny's face. 'I didn't know you were engaged,' she said, endeavouring to keep her voice steady.

'It's not official yet, so I'd rather you didn't say anything about it,' Gwen answered. 'We shall probably announce it at the New Year's Eve ball.'

Preparations were almost complete for this annual event to which everyone of note in the country was invited. In ordinary circumstances Jenny wouldn't have expected to take part but, as she would be still working at the manor, she presumed she would automatically join in with the festivities, and she had been looking forward to it with the keenest anticipation, but now she felt she would rather not go. It would be purgatory to have to listen to the announcement of Gwen and Nigel's engagement, to be obliged to watch the happy couple dancing joyously in each other's arms while she herself was left out in the cold.

If Gwen had been a different sort of person, steadfast and kind, and worthy of Nigel's love, Jenny wouldn't have minded quite so much, but it grieved her to think of him being married to such a selfish and vindictive girl. Having broken away from her once she couldn't understand how he could be so weak as to allow himself to be caught once more in her net. Didn't he realize she would stop at nothing to get what she wanted in life? That she would have no hesitation in cheating, and even lying, if it served her purpose?

As the morning wore on Jenny became increasingly nervous about seeing Nigel but, as it turned out, the meeting was less of an ordeal than she expected. His manner was perfectly pleasant, though perhaps a little more formal than usual, and he made no reference to their quarrel until after he had finished examining Mrs Ashcott. 'I would like her to have a complete rest for the next twelve hours,' he said, beckoning Jenny out of the room. 'It's only a precautionary measure but I know she's anxious to put in an appearance at the New Year's Eve ball and it would be a shame to disappoint her.'

'She seems quite bright and cheerful,' Jenny

said in a reserved tone of voice, 'but I will certainly keep her in bed for the rest of the day if you think it's advisable.'

He hesitated for a moment and, when he spoke, he sounded rather embarrassed. 'Look, Jenny,' he said. 'I'm sorry I behaved so badly last night. You have never given me any cause to question your dedication to the nursing profession and I had no right to haul you over the coals. I'm afraid I over reacted at seeing you with Alan.' Clearly he was under some kind of severe emotional stress but, by an iron effort of will, he held himself tightly under control. 'I hope you'll show you forgive me by saving some dances for me at the New Year's Eve ball,' he continued. 'Even if you intend to announce your engagement there's no necessity to spend the whole evening exclusively with my cousin.'

Jenny bit her lip. 'I've no intention of marrying Alan, at any rate until after I've finished my training,' she replied and she, too, had to make a conscious effort to keep her voice steady. 'Actually I didn't even know he was coming to the ball—I thought the invitations were reserved strictly for the upper crust.'

'Yes, I suppose that's true to a certain extent,' he agreed, 'but, as Gwen's future estate manager, Alan naturally qualifies for an invitation.'

Jenny's face lit up. 'Oh, I didn't know. Is the

appointment definite?' she asked.

'So I understand. Gwen tells me that Buckleigh has given Alan a thorough vetting and apparently he has passed with flying colours, so perhaps I have under-estimated my cousin. Married to the right girl he may yet turn out to be a worthwhile citizen.'

Jenny knew he found it difficult to praise Alan and she appreciated his generosity, though she little knew how much it cost him to speak well of the man he despised. 'I'm sure he'll make a splendid estate manager,' she said. 'It's just the incentive he needs. Thank you for telling me. You've really made my day.'

She walked with him as far as the front door and, after he had put on his coat, he lingered for a moment, eyeing her with some concern. 'You're looking tired,' he said, mistaking her look of strain for one of fatigue. 'It hasn't been too easy for you, working at the manor. I know there have been difficulties. But it won't be for much longer. I believe Miss Barraclough is taking over from you early next week.'

'I hope she'll stay,' Jenny replied rather doubtfully. 'It depends on whether she gets on with Mrs Paget.' 'And with Gwen,' she added to herself, though she thought it more tactful not to say this aloud.

'Fortunately there are hopeful signs that Mrs Ashcott may make a complete recovery,' Nigel told her. 'She's still a comparatively young woman so time is on her side and, as the paralysis is only partial, I see no reason why she should remain an invalid for the rest of her life. We must remember it's little more than three months since was taken ill, so it's early days yet.' Opening the front door he was greeted by a gust of cold wind and he glanced anxiously at the sky, where dark storm clouds were massing on the horizon. 'I'm afraid there's more rain on the way,' he said. 'The river's running dangerously high already, so we can only hope the banks will hold.'

Some of his anxiety communicated itself to Jenny. 'Isn't something being done about it?' she asked.

'Not enough,' he replied grimly. 'The water-board officials are never unduly concerned about the flooding of low-lying farmland. What they don't seem to realize is that there's more danger this year than ever before. Nature has a way of getting her own back and I wouldn't be surprised if the river finds its way back to its old course.'

Jenny gave an involuntary shiver. 'Which means good-bye to the Cottrells' cottage . . .' She left the rest of her sentence unsaid. 'Surely the family should be evacuated while there's still time?'

'Doris won't go of her own accord,' he reminded her, 'and the authorities won't forcibly evacuate her just because of possible danger. I'll be seeing Guy later today, so I'll have a word with him about it, and get him to send some farm hands over to the cottage with sandbags. That should help a little in case of an emergency, but it's not the answer.' He turned up his coat collar. 'Don't stand around in the cold, Jenny,' he said, and he gave her one of his rare smiles. 'I'll see you on New Year's Eve and don't forget to save me some dances.'

After he had gone she went back into the house, but she felt strangely restless and, finding Mrs Ashcott had fallen asleep, she wandered into the library and stood by the french windows, looking out at the bare, winter scene. Her thoughts were troubled, not only by reason of Doris and her family, but also by more personal problems.

Why had she been so reluctant to give Alan a definite answer, she wondered. 'Marriage is a big step,' she had told him. Yes, and so it was but, had it been an abyss, she would have bridged it in one leap if she truly loved him. She was fond of him and physically attracted to him, but she knew her feelings stemmed from the remembered love of a schoolgirl for a handsome boy, and his subsequent behaviour had done much to disillusion her.

Perhaps it was just as well she was going away, otherwise the announcement of Gwen and Nigel's engagement might drive her into Alan's arms and she didn't want to marry him for the wrong reasons. If, during her absence, he settled down in earnest to his new job, if he proved beyond doubt that he had sown his wild oats, if he stopped gambling, then perhaps she would feel happier about keeping the promise she had made under the kissing tree. But, for the moment, there were too many 'ifs' and, however forceful and demanding Alan proved to be, she was determined to stand by her decision to wait. It would be time enough to say 'yes' or 'no' when she had finished her training.

CHAPTER TEN

The rest of the day seemed endless and, to keep Mrs Ashcott amused, she spent the afternoon helping her to make decorations for the New Year's Eve ball. The holly and mistletoe, and the colourful paper chains, were still hanging in the hall, and Buckleigh and Pike had brought in a plentiful supply of ivy for Mrs Paget and Mrs Pike to entwine round the pillars. Hundreds of fairy lights still had to be hung and Jenny thought it would be an improvement if little Christmas bushes were put in the windows, so she showed Mrs Ashcott how to decorate small embroidery hoops with furze and evergreens. As a final touch she brightened them up with oranges and apples and even Gwen admired the finished product.

'Quite pretty and very original,' she praised. 'You seem to have an artistic touch. I suppose you wouldn't like to help Mrs Paget and Mrs Pike with the pillar decorations in the hall? They're a bit ham-fisted and, in the old days, Mother always supervised everything and made tactful suggestions.'

'Why can't *you* lend a hand?' Jenny wondered, but Gwen was so occupied with fittings and rehearsals she hadn't a spare moment.

However, Jenny had no objection to masterminding the decorations and she found Mrs Paget most co-operative and helpful. Mrs Pike, on the other hand, seemed surly and resentful, and Jenny wondered why the woman had taken such a dislike to her.

'What have I done to upset her?' she asked, when she and Mrs Paget had a few minutes alone together. 'She's most unfriendly.'

The housekeeper looked uncomfortable. 'Oh, you don't have to take any notice of her,' she said. 'Emmie Pike was born miserable.'

But Jenny knew this wasn't true. She had seen Mrs Paget and Mrs Pike laughing together, and the caretaker's wife was obviously on good terms with Buckleigh, joking and back-chatting with him in the friendliest possible way. No, she herself must have done something to annoy the woman, though what it was she couldn't imagine.

However, it wasn't a bit of good to worry about it because Mrs Paget was obviously not going to enlighten her.

When Shirley arrived the next morning, to help her mother and the housekeeper with the final preparations for the ball, the unfriendly atmosphere was even more noticeable and Jenny kept out of the kitchen as much as possible. Caterers had been called in to take charge of the buffet supper which was being provided for the guests, but there was still plenty of work for the household domestics to do and, as Shirley was enjoying a break from work, the paint factory being closed for more than a week to cover the Christmas and New Year holidays, Mrs Pike had roped her in to give a helping hand.

When Jenny went into the kitchen to fetch Mrs Ashcott's 'elevenses', the chatter between the three women dried up like a tap being turned off, and it was so embarrassing that she herself remained silent, and she made her escape as quickly as possible. As lunchtime approached she had to steel herself to go into the kitchen again, but this time only Shirley was there and she decided to pretend she hadn't noticed anything amiss.

'Is Mrs Ashcott's lunch ready?' she asked, putting a clean cloth on the invalid's tray. Shirley jerked her head in the direction of the Aga stove, where a fillet of Dover sole was steaming between two plates, but she made no attempt to get up from the table where she was sitting with a magazine propped in front of her. A feeling of irritation swept over Jenny. 'Why aren't you helping your mother and Mrs Paget?' she asked.

'They're doing the upstairs,' Shirley answered. 'I said I'd keep an eye on the dinner, though I don't see it's any of your business.'

Jenny bit her lip. The girl was being deliberately rude, but there must be a reason for her behaviour and she wanted to find out what it was. 'I suppose you come up to the manor every year to help with the preparations for the New Year's Eve ball,' she said. 'Have you lived at the lodge all your life?'

Shirley nodded. 'I was born there,' she replied and there was a note of pride in her voice. 'There's been Pikes at the lodge almost as long as there's been Ashcotts at the manor. We belong here, just as much as the Ashcotts, and I don't *ever* want to leave. One time there was talk of Charlie Buckleigh taking over as estate manager when Mr Buckleigh retired and Mum was all for me marrying him, but I didn't fancy him all that much and anyway he's joined the army now.'

Jenny smiled. 'Well, I don't suppose you'll have much difficulty in finding somebody to take his place,' she remarked. The girl was really pretty, rather like Gwen, with the same gipsy-black hair and startling blue eyes.

Indeed, the resemblance was so marked they could almost have been cousins, and was this so very surprising? If, in the past, the Ashcott girls had slept with Kings, then it was more than likely the men had slept around too, and it wasn't beyond the realms of possibility that the caretaker's daughter had more than a drop of Ashcott blood in her veins.

Shirley tossed her head. 'I'm not marrying just anyone,' she said. 'I can afford to be choosey, but happen I haven't got quite the advantages of *some* people.' The resentment in her eyes as she cast a glance at Jenny from under her long lashes, was unmistakable. 'I wasn't brought up to be a lady and I mightn't be thought good enough in some circles. All the same, I was getting along fine with Alan Wickham till *you* came along.'

So that was it. It was out in the open at last and, in a strange sort of way, it was a relief to Jenny to know the truth. Shirley had probably always been in love with Alan and, now that he was going to be the new estate manager, she was understandably more attracted to him than ever. No wonder she resented Jenny, who appeared to pose a threat to her future plans.

'You needn't worry, Shirley,' Jenny said, suddenly realizing she had already made up her mind. 'I'm not going to marry Alan, if that's what you're afraid of. I did think about it quite seriously at one time but I've come to the conclusion we aren't right for each other.

You'll make him a much better wife and I wish you joy with all my heart.' Impulsively she gave the younger girl a hug, and she was surprised and touched by the younger girl's ready response.

'Anyway, he's not good enough for you,' Shirley declared. 'I know Alan through and through and I'll take him as I find him, faults and all, which is more than you would have done. Mind you, he's not asked me yet but he'll come round to it in the end. I've watched him go around with first one girl and then another but you were the only one he was ever serious about and, as soon as you've given him his marching orders, he'll come homing back to me, because I'm right for him and he knows it. Once I've got his ring on my finger I won't put up with any nonsense from him, and he'll never break my heart the way he'd have broken yours.'

Jenny knew the girl was speaking nothing less than the truth. Had she herself married Alan he would continually have gone astray, but Shirley was a realist who had no time for romantic dreams. She loved Alan, despite his faults, and her strength of character was such that she would make him toe the line. In fact, marrying Shirley would probably be his salvation and Jenny was glad she had found the strength to bow out gracefully, and she wished them both the best of luck.

It remained to be seen whether she would

be able to bear the announcement of Gwen and Nigel's engagement with equal fortitude, and it was with a heavy heart that she got ready for the New Year's Eve ball.

First she had to play lady-in-waiting to Mrs Ashcott and, with loving kindness, she dressed the lady of the manor in the beautiful ball gown she had worn the previous year. It had been arranged that she would sit in her wheelchair at the foot of the staircase, with Gwen by her side, and greet the guests as they arrived. Then it would be Jenny's duty to stay with her till she grew weary, after which Mrs Paget would take over and remain in charge of the invalid for the rest of the evening, leaving Jenny free to take part in the festivities.

It took much longer to get Mrs Ashcott ready than Jenny had expected and time was running out when at last she was able to attend to herself. Fortunately she had already laid out her clothes on her bed and she collected everything and rushed upstairs to have a quick bath.

There was no full-length mirror downstairs so, when she came out of the bathroom, she paused outside Gwen's bedroom and, after a moment's hesitation, she tapped on the half open door. The light was on but the room was empty, so she took a hurried look at herself in the long mirror before going over to the dressing-table to view her hair style from all angles in the triple mirror. As she did so, her glance happened to rest on a large framed photograph which stood in a place of honour among the clutter of powder boxes and lipsticks. It was an enlargement of a garden snapshot of Gwen and Nigel. Standing by the sundial with their arms linked together, the camera had caught them in a happy moment. Gwen was laughing and Nigel was looking young and carefree and very much in love.

A pain, such as she had never felt before, gripped Jenny's heart before she realized this must be an old photograph, taken during the previous year when the happy couple were newly engaged. But her relief was short-lived because she knew the renewal of their engagement was imminent and, before this very evening was over, Gwen would once more be able to flaunt Nigel's ring on the third finger of her left hand.

Gwen met her as she came downstairs. 'Where *have* you been?' she demanded crossly. 'I've been looking all over for you. You're supposed to be in charge of Mother and you know perfectly well the first guests are due to arrive at any moment.'

'Mrs Ashcott is quite ready,' Jenny responded, forbearing to point out that she herself had had a bare twenty minutes in which to get bathed and changed.

'I don't know what's happened to Nigel either,' Gwen fretted, glancing impatiently at the antique clock which hung in an alcove beside the enormous hearth, where huge yule logs were burning. 'I particularly asked him to get here early in case Mother needed a tranquillizer or something. Still, I suppose being kept waiting is something I shall have to put up with if I'm to be a doctor's wife.'

She sounded far more keyed-up than the occasion warranted. After all, there had been New Year's Eve balls at the manor as far back as she could remember, and she was well used to public appearances. Could it be that Nigel hadn't come up to scratch after all, and was she upset because the announcement of her engagement was going to be delayed? This might account for her being so jittery, especially as she had been foolish enough to have already told Jenny she was unofficially engaged to Nigel.

The bell rang at that moment and Gwen flew to open the door and let Nigel in. Rain could be seen, pouring down in torrents and making a waterfall of the front steps. 'Your guests will have to leave their cars and come by boat if this rain goes on for much longer,' he remarked, shrugging off his wet coat and stamping his feet on the mat. 'The first lord of the manor knew what he was doing when he built his house on a hill. He was making sure that, even if the whole valley flooded, the Ashcotts would remain snug and dry in their own particular Noah's ark.' Jenny was still standing at the bottom of the stairs, wishing that she, instead of Gwen, could have been the one to run forward and greet him, and his glance rested on her a trifle longer than was necessary, causing her heart to miss a beat. ‘How is Mrs Ashcott?’ he asked. ‘I’d better go and see her before the party begins.’

Gwen linked her arm in his. ‘Doesn’t Jenny look nice?’ she said in a condescending voice. ‘I always say if you find a dress you like you might as well wear it till it falls to pieces.’

In fact, this was only the second time Jenny had worn the dress, the other occasion being on Christmas Eve, but it was Gwen’s nature to be catty, so Jenny ignored the rather stupid remark and, with her head held high, she led the way in Mrs Ashcott’s bedroom.

The invalid was sitting in an armchair and Mrs Paget was fussing round her, holding up a hand mirror so that she could see how nicely Jenny had arranged her pretty, white hair. She smiled at Nigel and nodded her head when he asked her if she was feeling well enough to undertake her duties as hostess. All that was required of her was to sit in her wheelchair and greet the guests as they arrived, but he feared the unaccustomed excitement might prove too much for her, and he instructed Jenny to hover in the vicinity and wheel her back to her room if she showed any sign of stress.

However, long years of training stood Mrs Ashcott in good stead and Jenny found herself silently agreeing with Nigel who had remarked that the lady had style. Gwen might be more arrestingly beautiful but, when it came to regal behaviour, she couldn't hold a candle to her mother.

Presently the last of the guests arrived, and the orchestra, which had been playing background music, now began tuning up for the first dance. Gwen looked around for Jenny and, with an imperious nod of the head, she indicated that it was time for Mrs Ashcott to leave the party. Jenny obediently wheeled the invalid away and, looking back over her shoulder, she saw Gwen making a bee-line in Nigel's direction. Whether or not the engagement was going to be announced this evening, she was clearly determined that everyone present should get the message—Nigel was her property and the broken romance was definitely on again.

When Jenny returned to the ballroom the festivities were well under way and Alan was impatiently waiting for her. They hadn't met since the other night when he had tried to force her into agreeing to marry him and, remembering how they had been interrupted by Nigel storming into the farm kitchen, he eyed her a trifle warily.

'I was sorry about Mrs Ashcott's fall,' he said, taking her hand and leading her out onto the crowded floor. 'Fortunately she doesn't seem to be any the worse for it.'

'No thanks to you,' she retorted. 'The consequences might have been tragic and Nigel was furious with me for not getting back at the proper time.'

'Nigel thinks he's God Almighty,' Alan growled. 'Actually, I believe he was more furious about finding us kissing than he was about Mrs Ashcott being neglected. Look, Jenny,' he added, 'I haven't pestered you for the past few days, but when are you going to make up your mind about marrying me? I've pulled every string I can think of and I've managed to land this job as estate manager, so I can offer you a decent home and security—what more do you want?'

'I know, Alan. Nigel told me. It's splendid news and I do congratulate you.' She hesitated, looking at him with genuine affection. If only they could turn back the clock and be boy and girl again, plighting their troth under the kissing tree. Everything had been so simple and straightforward in those days, but time doesn't stand still and they had both grown up. The type of man Alan had become didn't appeal to her and, if she married him, she would spend all her time nagging and fault finding. For both their sakes it would be better to end it now, and it would be easier for Alan than it would be for her, because he would soon console himself with Shirley, while she herself had no one to fill the gap. Fortunately she had a new job to look forward to and she was determined to throw herself heart and soul into the nursing profession.

'You're turning me down, aren't you?' he said, rightfully construing the reason for her silence. 'What am I supposed to do now? Go out and shoot myself?'

This was so typical of Alan that she couldn't help laughing. 'Nothing so drastic,' she told him. 'Why not have a word with Shirley Pike and see what she advises? I think you'll find her far more co-operative than I am.'

His face flushed a dull red. 'So she's been talking, has she?' he asked. 'I might have guessed. She surely doesn't expect me to marry her, just because I've kissed her and cuddled her a few times. God's truth, I never meant it to go as far as it did, but you've been so infuriating, Jenny, blowing first hot and then cold and, as I've told you before, I'm no saint.'

'Think it over, Alan,' she coaxed. 'Shirley will make you a good wife and she belongs here on the Ashcott estate, which is another point in her favour.'

'I suppose you're right,' he said gloomily, 'but I don't think much of the way you keep your promises. You seem to have forgotten the kissing tree.'

'I'm not the little girl I used to be, and you're not the little boy,' she reminded him. She spoke lightly but the bold look he gave her in return brought the colour to her cheeks.

'You're too right,' he whispered meaningly

and, before she realized what he was doing, he manoeuvred her between the other dancing couples towards the library, which he rightly guessed would be empty.

The door was ajar and he kicked it open with the back of his heel, holding her so tightly in his arms that she couldn't escape without making a scene. Once the door was shut she tried desperately to break away from him, but he continued to hold her in a vice-like grip and his kisses were so violent they frightened her. He had never behaved quite like this before and it took the sharp, insistent ringing of the telephone on the table behind him to bring him to his senses. With a muttered oath he released her and she snatched up the receiver and held it for a moment like a weapon to keep him at bay.

Cynthia's voice came crackling over the air and Jenny put the receiver to her ear while Alan backed out of the room, clearly in a villainous temper. Jenny laughed a little shakily. 'Saved by the bell for the second time,' she said to herself, and she took a deep breath in order to steady her pulse rate. 'Cynthia?' she asked. 'Yes, it's me—Jenny. Whatever's the matter? You sound all het up.'

'You sound a bit overwrought yourself,' Cynthia replied, 'or is it just the party spirit? Actually I'm ringing up about little Linda Cottrell. She seems to be having some sort of asthmatic attack, and Doris has panicked and sent Cliff over here to ask us if we can get in touch with Nigel. I hate to ask him to turn out in the middle of a party, especially on a night like this, but it sounds really serious. Guy has gone back to the cottage with Cliff, but he can't do much except try and calm Doris down, so do you think Nigel would mind coming to the rescue? I'm afraid the weather's absolutely diabolical—Cliff got soaked to the skin coming here on his motor bike.'

'Yes, I'm sure he'll come,' Jenny told her. 'Gwen will be livid but that can't be helped. She told me a few days ago she was hoping to announce her engagement this evening, but she can hardly do so if Nigel goes missing.'

Cynthia chuckled. 'Well, that's one bright spot anyway. The longer it's put off the better. Do you think you could fetch Nigel to the phone? I'd better have a word with him.'

Nigel was dancing with Monica Dewfall, one of the Plumpton Players, and he didn't seem particularly upset about being dragged away from her. Jenny hurriedly explained the situation and then followed him into the library. While he spoke to Cynthia she went over to the french windows and drew aside the curtain, but it was a dark and windy night and she could see nothing except the heavy rain which was beating against the house with ever-increasing fury. Its violence frightened her and she turned quickly as he put down the receiver.

'Nigel—take care,' she said and, in that

brief, unguarded moment, she betrayed herself, for there was no mistaking the expression on her face, and the tender, loving concern in her voice. In two strides he crossed the room and swept her into his arms.

'My love . . . My dearest dear,' he murmured, and his mouth came down on hers in a kiss so ardent, and yet so tender, it exceeded her wildest dreams.

They were disturbed by a movement at the door and, turning, they saw Gwen standing on the threshold, her eyes blazing in a face drained of colour. 'I'm sorry to interrupt such a touching scene,' she said in a furious voice, 'but Monica says you've had a call to go and see Linda Cottrell.' She looked meaningly at their clasped hands. 'Judging by your behaviour there doesn't seem to be any particular urgency, so you surely don't intend to leave the party for such a trivial reason?'

'I wouldn't say it was a trivial reason,' Nigel replied, looking extremely annoyed by the interruption. 'Linda happens to be a very delicate child who could easily die without prompt medical attention.'

'But you can't go out in weather like this,' Gwen insisted. 'Mrs Paget has been listening to the local radio and a warning has just gone out that the river may burst its banks within the next half-hour.'

'Then the sooner I go the better,' he responded. He brushed Jenny's cheek gently with the tips of his fingers. 'I'll be back for "Auld Lang Syne",' he promised, 'so be sure to save the last dance for me.'

But it was long after midnight before he returned and, in the interim, Jenny died a thousand deaths, fully believing she would never see him again, because it was less than five minutes after his departure that the warning sirens sounded, and she knew this meant that the river had burst its banks. If the main road flooded, Nigel and his car would be swept to destruction and no power on eath could save him. Desperately she clung to the hope that he would reach the cottage in time to take refuge in the upstair rooms with the other occupants until help arrived.

Marooned on the hill, there was nothing that anyone at the manor could do to assist with the rescue operations, so the dancing continued as if nothing had happened. In fact many of the guests were unaware of the catastrophe and, as in previous years, the rafters rang to the music of 'Auld Lang Syne'.

Later there was a phone call from the authorities, urgently requesting permission to use the manor as a temporary accommodation for some of the homeless and injured, because the road to the hospital was impassable, and the rest centre was already filled to overflowing.

Towards dawn the survivors began to trickle in: crying children who had become separated from their parents: whole families who had lost their homes and their belongings. Cold and shocked, they needed hot drinks and blankets, and many required medical attention. Jenny was glad to be kept busy. It prevented her from thinking about what might have happened to Nigel and Guy and the Cottrell family.

She was bandaging a woman's injured arm when she glanced up and saw Doris and Joe being shepherded through the front door by a St John's ambulance man. Doris was carrying Linda, and Joe held Benjy in one arm and Harry in the other, while Cliff brought up the rear, carrying the few belongings they had managed to salvage from the flood. There was no sign of Guy or Nigel, and Jenny's heart dropped like a stone.

She finished tying the bandage and then went across to speak to Doris, first enquiring about Linda, before asking for news of the two missing men.

Doris told her that Linda was better, thanks to the injection Nigel had given her, and she thankfully handed over the little girl to Jenny who said she would undress her and wrap her in warm blankets.

'Guy went back to the farm to see if Cynthia was all right, but I don't know what happened to Doctor Barrett,' Doris added. 'The last time I saw him he was up to his waist in water, carrying a child to safety.' Her eyes shone with admiration. 'He's a real hero, is Doctor Barrett. If you ask me, he deserves a medal.'

Jenny's spirits lifted a little. At least there was a chance that her loved one was still alive and, when she had attended to Linda, she carried the child over to the window to admire the Christmas bushes. Morning had broken and the newly risen sun was shining in a blaze of glory, turning the water-logged drive into a ribbon of gold. 'Look, Linda,' she said. 'There's a rainbow.'

The bridge of promise soared in a splendid arc, spanning the western sky with colours as clear and bright as those found in a child's paintbox. Even as she watched, two hands were laid gently on her shoulders, and very softly Nigel's voice sang the first lines of the 'Rainbow Song'.

She put Linda down, telling her to go and find Doris, and then she turned to look at the man she loved. He was unshaven and soaked to the skin but he was her 'Mr Wonderful'.

'Kiss me,' she said, smiling into his eyes.

He smiled back at her. 'I was going to,' he answered, laughter spilling to the surface as he swept her into his arms. 'You didn't need to ask.'